The Delicate Ape

Dorothy B. Hughes

An Orion book

Copyright © Dorothy B. Hughes 1944

This edition published by
The Orion Publishing Group Ltd
Orion House
5 Upper St Martin's Lane
London WC2H 9EA

An Hachette UK company
A CIP catalogue record for this book is available from the British Library

ISBN 978 1 4719 1733 2

www.orionbooks.co.uk

For Abbot Leonard Schwinn
'In Viam Pacis'

I

The man came out of the front doors of the great and gray Pennsylvania Station into the early night. The street was curiously empty, deserted. It was as if all living, moving things had known he was emerging at this hour and this place and had, in instinct rather than knowledge, scuttled into hiding. The lighted lamps at the moment seemed to throw no black geometrics to the pavement. Rather there was spread a strange twilight look, not light, not dark, an unhealthy pallor. Far overhead the sky was clear. If you looked long enough and hard enough you could distinguish the fragments of stars.

The man started across the wide deserted street to the opposite pavement. His heels counted his steps with fearsome clarity. In the silence, intensified by the muted hum of uptown New York, they had the sound of doom. They were too even, too studied; he should break the rhythm, perhaps run the last of the way. He did not run. He was afraid to run, a fear perhaps if once he started he would not be able to stop.

He stood for a moment listening, not moving. The night touched a chill finger to the back of his neck and the touch snaked down his spine into his entrails. It wasn't a cold night but Washington had been humid, unseasonably so for May; the club car had been, despite conditioning, airless. The contrast was too sudden for his blood to warm before he shivered. He thrust his hands into his pockets and started towards Broadway.

There was no taxi in sight; he hadn't expected there would be. If he'd wanted one, he could have moved with the other passengers towards the underground stands rather than making his way through the station and out the front door. The walk would be good for him. He needed air in his lungs. The blocks to the hotel, where he had registered four days earlier, were short, too short for a man who normally covered miles in a day. He had spent hours sitting in offices and trains this day; he was tired of the indoors and inaction.

He bit on the truth. He was afraid to take a cab. Cab drivers were open to bribery. Even if he were delivered safely, there could afterwards be a whispered conference on the corner, an exchange of address for a dirty green bill. He would walk. One of the occupants of the club car conceivably might have known that the man in the dark blue suit and brown shoes and soft brown hat, the youngish man without distinguishing marks, was Piers Hunt.

Conceivably in one or another of the government offices where he, as Mr. Thompson—Smith, Brown, Jones were too obvious—had wasted the day, someone might have divined his true identity. How, he didn't know. He hadn't a half dozen speaking acquaintances in this part of the world. He had seen none of them since he arrived. Piers Hunt was not known to be in the United States; he had no reason to be here. The job on this side of the water was Gordon's. Even Gordon didn't have information that Piers had come over. But Piers knew that there were times when inaccessible knowledge filtered through in almost fanciful fashion. This might be one of them.

He turned left, started up the cavernous empty path of mid Broadway. The lights here, not many blocks from the sunburst of Times Square, were sparse, and the overhanging heights of buildings laid heavier shadow than was pleasant. There was no reason to be uneasy, listening to the hard metre of his heels thudding the pavement. He had been alone in front of the Pennsylvania.

There was a loneness more pregnant of danger than sight or smell of the enemy. It was a loneness he had known in jungle deeps and in forest, moments when it seemed as if God had withdrawn His hand. There was no reason for the feeling to enter into him here but it quivered within him. Its very reasonlessness quickened his senses and he divined rather than heard the footsteps behind him.

They were not close, not as yet, and they were not loud. They were more indistinct than the city sound a few scant leagues ahead of him. They might have been imaginary, but when he broke the rhythm of his stride, diminishing it, he heard them, distinct. He walked a few paces then again broke rhythm and again he heard them falter in their attempt to synchronize into invisibility. He knew then, knew this was no casual walker on the streets of New York.

He controlled the impulse to break and run. The kaleidoscope of lights was visible ahead but he was only at 36th street. He knew how far Times Square lay in actuality. He might, it was true, be able to outrun his pursuer these blocks but he couldn't hope to outdistance a bullet. That he had not been killed before he became conscious of the follower became a latent reassurance. This man, whoever he was, wasn't hired to kill, only to smell out the burrow where the fox was holed. With the realization came quick hard anger, and, on its heels, decision.

They didn't know the hotel where he was registered. They weren't to learn this easily. Having discarded the first method of escape, a sprint, he also discarded the next obvious, a devious route. His anger at being discovered was too sharp. Had there been other men abroad on this lonely stretch, he would have faded into the shawl of a facade, waited to surprise his shadow. But all humans, save himself and the man in the dark behind him, were still hiding where they had fled at the silent crackling of danger. He did what he dared out of anger, out of hopelessness akin to despair, out of spirit. He turned, stood planted, hands shoved deep into the pockets of his dark sack coat. He stood, a target, and waited.

The man behind him didn't know what to do. The man, had his nerves been strong, could have turned on his heel and slunk away. Instead he moved, hesitant, his steps lagging as he cowered forward the more than half-block to where Piers waited. He came al-

4

most abreast and Piers did not give way. He stopped then. He was a small man, a head and half smaller than Piers. His coat was bunchy, his new dove-gray hat sat stiffly on his head. There was a small green feather stuck in the bow. His face was a yellowish square; he wore a bedraggled yellow mustache over bad teeth, and his pale eyes were shifty under ragged yellow eyebrows. His necktie was stiff and ugly, in purples and greens. There was a greenish tinge to his brown suit.

Piers didn't see this detail on the dark street. The man had been across the aisle, near to the door, in the club car up from Washington. A man rolling a thin cigarette, rubbing at a spot on his black shoes, scraping his thumb nail on his chin—a man with nervous fingers. The eyes scuttled now from Piers. He dived right. Piers shifted inexorably. A scribble of terror went over the yellow face. A tongue licked the lips, the eyes measured the space to the left.

Piers spoke softly, so softly. "Have you a match?"

The tongue darted out again; the glands of the man's thin neck swelled.

"A match," Piers repeated. He kept his eyes on the face before him.

The man started to tremble, it began with his hat and ran through him like water. The nervous fingers fumbled in his pockets. His eyes kept leaping to Piers' jacket pocket; jammed stiffly forward by his fingers. He didn't say a word.

Piers laughed so softly. His voice blurred. "Or have you the time, perhaps?"

Terror jabbed into the man. His fingers, shaking

like wind, held a small packet of unwanted matches.

"You have a match," Piers noted gently. "Strike one."

The craven obeyed. His tongue kept touching the corners of his mouth. The trembling light flared.

"Hold it higher," Piers suggested. "No, higher."

It illumined the yellow face, the perspiration wetting the brow and the scraggling yellow mustache, the moisture in the nostrils, the frantic eyes.

Piers blew his breath and they were again in darkness. "I wanted to see your face." He said it pleasantly but still too softly. He waited but the man did not, could not speak. "Shall we walk together now?" He swung beside the man and his arm jarred the shaking elbow. "It is wiser, perhaps. There might be danger walking alone these dark blocks. I take it you are going my way?"

The man stumbled forward, pressed on by Piers' dominant arm. He didn't make any sound but his breathing was like a sob. Obviously he believed that Piers held a gun. Obviously he himself did not carry one, or, if he did, dared not reach for it. They crossed to where the Metropolitan Opera House stood, dark, deserted after the season. In this abandoned block the man, if he were a man, would turn and strike. He wasn't. He was as boneless as inert matter.

Knowing this, yet because of the possibility of attack, Piers spoke again. "What is your name?"

The breathing thickened. The man was trying to speak but only sounds came.

Piers repeated, "Your name. What is your name?"

6

The voice came at last. It was thin, reedy. "Where are you taking me? What do you want with me?"

Piers laughed. It wasn't meant to reassure. He said, "I told you. I believe it is safer we walk the rest of the way together. And what is your name?"

"What do you want with me?" the man stammered shrilly.

"You were on the train from Washington," Piers said. "I noticed you. Did you know that I noticed you, Mr. . . . ?"

The man said eagerly, as if it were a lesson well learned, "I am a commercial traveler. Between New York and Washington. I live in New York."

Piers interrupted. "In this country you are called a traveling salesman." His voice laughed. "You should have been told that, too. Perhaps we can have a drink together. There are some questions I should like to put to you. Your name. Your—"

They had come upon 42nd street. Across it flared the white and red and green and blue lights of a bright Broadway. Once it had been blacked out. That was a long time ago, twelve and more years ago. Returning to it after twelve years, Piers could not look upon the whiteness without a welling in his blood, a determination in his heart. The lights of the world, the lights of Broadway, must not be put out again.

Still jabbing the hireling's elbow, he moved him across the street to the west side where the brightest lights overhung the pavement below. The walk was dense with man, the customary, evening, before-theater crowd, milling and swelling and shuffling north and south. Beyond the curb the motor traffic was as dense as the foot traffic here, and more strident —the hard rub of tires, the squeal of brakes, the whir of motors. The hum of the city rose to a percussive din; there were no shadows in the electric glare.

Piers bent to the ear of his captive. "Why won't you tell me your name? I can find out, you know."

They were in front of the Paramount where the crowd was most thick, the noise most shrill, pierced only by the atonal chant of the theater's uniformed barker, . . . *seatsinside* . . . *seats inside* . . .

Without warning the man ducked and cut away. Piers, turning quickly, saw his bunchy coat pushing frantically through the mass, battering against its imperturbability and its ingrained dislike of a disturbing cross-current. Piers shouted, "Wait—"

The man heard him, his head half-turned, and the fear on it illumined the dark mass where momentarily he was arrested. He plunged again out of sight and Piers again shouted, "Wait—" He himself battered through the crowd, making his way to the curb where he could both see ahead and move more quickly. The man had done the same. Yet he might have lost himself amidst the dark coats and the pale, feathered hats had he not looked over his shoulder again. He saw Piers coming after him; he must have seen the impossibility of escape. His mouth opened but whatever sound came out was lost in the noise of the city. The man looked back again and he plunged off the curb into the onrushing propulsion of traffic.

There was the agonized scream of braking; there was the sudden roar of wonder from the crowd before it pressed ravenously towards this human sacrifice. In the moment when the mob stood awed, before it moved, Piers saw the mashed thing. Before the quick blast of the police whistle shrilled nearer, Piers had mingled with the northbound stream of walkers again. There was no need to remain to give testimony. Too many were there who could repeat, "He jumped in front of the cab." There was no need to remain to hear the inevitable evidence of someone who had noticed, "A man was chasing him."

What manner of man? A tall man in a dark suit. The streets were crowded with small men, middling men, tall men in dark suits.

Piers sauntered on without looking back. He crossed 44th street; he moved steadily, without outward evidence of the turmoil blackening his inward heart. He had sent a second man to meet death.

2.

There were red-mouthed women and waxed men on the shallow steps of the Astor. Piers walked through them into the lobby. It was crowded as always before theater time, afternoon and night, and after theater. It was seldom without its hosts and it was seldom that the same face appeared successively. The meeting place of the Forties, of Broadway. Piers had chosen it for precisely this transient quality, remembered from the past, unchanged in the present.

Music from the dining room floated to the lobby below. Perfume and fresh flowers and barber lotions spilled from the mezzanine. There was constant motion, incessant sound, and anonymity. Piers didn't go directly to the desk for his key. He joined the unhurried motion of the lobby, seeking without seeming to seek a face which did not belong here, a face that might match the one now lying under the cabbie's tire. He saw none.

His nerves hadn't quieted; his blood churned from the encounter and its ruthless end. He would have a drink before going upstairs. It wasn't that he feared to be alone; he wanted to be alone to think, but he was afraid of thinking unless he could dull the edge of thought. He walked towards the bar and he saw, slanted in the doorway there, Gordon. He knew then it was too late for thinking. What had happened tonight was not only inevitable, it was no longer of import. Gordon saw him. Gordon had been waiting for him. The man opened his eyes in surprised recognition and he held out his hand as Piers reached the open doorway.

"My God, Hunt," he said. "What are you doing here? I didn't believe it at first but it's you, all right."

"It's I," Piers said. He took the firm clasp. Gordon looked fit, handsome and competent as always. Without Piers' height, he was still the more commanding figure, perhaps because of his military shoulders, the well-constructed bulk. Gordon always looked his best. He was face-handsome too. A good oblong face with strong chin, a dark well-clipped mustache over his rich mouth, dark blue eyes under straight brows, dark hair curling just enough above the broad tanned forehead. Women liked Gordon. Men liked him more perhaps. He was a man's man. Women were for the hours when work didn't press. Gordon's life was strong and ordered. Piers had never envied him more than he did in this moment of meeting at the Astor Bar.

Gordon said, "But I thought you were to hold the line in Berne?"

"I wasn't needed," Piers told him. "Nickerson had returned from Istanbul and Wiles was there. They know the mechanics better than I. I particularly wanted to be in on this conference and I jumped at the chance to come, although unofficially." He smiled. He knew his smile, not sure of itself like Gordon's, a little smile, tentative.

"I'd have jumped at the chance to miss it." Gordon smiled his smile. "I've always thought you lucky to be the field assistant while I had to stay in Washington and listen to talk." He split a hammered red-gold cigarette case, heavy with monogram, passed it.

Piers refused. He had a like case; both were gifts from the Secretary. He never carried his. It was too rich for his blood. It belonged in Gordon's hand. Gordon touched a gold lighter. "Did you travel with the old man?"

Piers said, "I said good-by to him in Alex. I flew to Berne. It was only after I found Nickerson there that I decided to come over." He added, but it was to himself, "I haven't been home in twelve years."

Gordon took a whiff of his Turkish cigarette.

Piers laughed softly. "He doesn't know I'm here." His brows drew together. "I tried to find him this afternoon in Washington but he wasn't in."

Gordon threw away the cigarette. He said, "He hasn't arrived."

Piers allowed a startled look to meet Gordon's steady one.

"We're explaining the delay—but only to those who must know—by saying that he had business in South America."

"No," Piers said. He said it again, shaking his head. "No. One of us would have known."

Gordon asked with a pitiful eagerness, "Did you see him on the plane? With whom was he flying?"

"I put him on the plane myself," Piers answered. He added slowly, steadily, "I didn't know the pilot. I'd never seen him before."

They stood there in silence, in the midst of sound. Piers broke through it. "I came in for a drink. Join me. I've just seen a man killed."

Gordon started. He settled his shoulders again before he followed Piers into the undersea light of the room, past close-set tables to the crowded bar. He said, "I can't accept death as casually as you, Piers. It always gets my nerves. I suppose you learned its unimportance in combat service while I learned nothing sitting in Washington, adding up figures with one hand and saluting brass hats with the other."

Piers said, "Rye," to the barman.

"I'll stick to Scotch and splash," Gordon said.

Piers turned to face him. "Death is often casual, Gordon. This one was. The man leaped in front of a traveling cab. A strange little man in a misfit coat and a new hat. The hat wasn't touched. But the mustache was. It wasn't much of a mustache. A ragged yellow affair." He lifted his glass.

Gordon spoke with a tremor. "You looked at him."

Piers swallowed the rye neat. "It happened he was in my car coming up from Washington." He lit a cigarette from his crumpled package. "It isn't often that you see a second time someone you halfway notice in a restaurant or on a train. It's casual." He pushed his glass again to the barman.

Gordon said, "I don't have your nerves, Piers. I'd be home in bed after an encounter like that." He smiled his particular smile. "Hoping the Clootie hadn't followed."

Piers met his smile. "He looked like a commercial traveler. Nothing important. He didn't look at all the sort of man who was traveling in Samarra."

Gordon put down his glass unevenly.

"Someone in the crowd said a man was chasing him. But he got away. Another drink?"

Gordon touched a white linen handkerchief to his mustache. "Sorry. I'm with a party. I shouldn't have taken this long." He folded the handkerchief away. "It can't be that anything's happened to the old man. There've been no unaccounted plane accidents reported. He must have stopped over somewhere."

"Not without telling us," Piers said.

"There's not a week before the conclave opens."

"What will happen if he doesn't come by then?"

Gordon spoke thoughtfully. "The President will appoint an acting secretary."

"One of us."

"Yes." His face was grave. "One of us." He had no doubt as to which one it would be.

Neither had Piers. He paid the check, started away from the bar.

Gordon halted him. "Where can I reach you? Where are you stopping?"

"The Plaza. I'll ring you in the morning."

They separated; he continued to the door. If Gordon tried to reach him there, he'd insist he'd said Savoy-Plaza. At the door, he paused, turning to allow the woman in iridescent feathers to pass him. Standing there he could watch Gordon rejoin his table. It was set where it commanded the door and the corridor outside. For the moment his heart was constricted. And then his eyes cleared and he saw it wasn't she whom he feared it was. It was a young girl with hair pale lavender in this light, dark purple eyes and a shimmering violet dress.

There were also at the table two quite ordinary young men. Disbelieving in the normal, he concentrated in that brief moment on the men. Neither looked as if he would recognize the jaundiced commercial traveler as a part of the human race. Each wore the face of Princeton or Yale, handsome, sure, protected. Gordon must have looked that way when he was young, during the war when he was at a desk in Washington, aide-de-camp to an important—socially and politically—Major General. Gordon hadn't lived in the land of death. He had never known the descent to hell, the stench of human decay in his nostrils, the rivers of blood lapping his boots.

He was watching Piers from the table. Piers moved

as soon as the feathered one's attendants had passed him and he turned outside the door as if he were seeking the 44th street exit. He waited for a moment in that corridor but no one came after him, and, avoiding the bar doorway, he made his way by the back corridor to the desk.

The sleek-haired clerk with the scent of dark carnation said, "No messages, Mr. Pierce." He passed across the key.

Piers scowled at it on his hand. He didn't want the clerk to identify face with name; this was the first evening that it had happened. He took the papers from the newsstand, added a pack of cigarettes, and went to the elevators. No one was standing on watch; the activity of the hotel, intensified as curtain time grew nearer, was centered in the front lobby. Piers waited until the elevator cage was shut before he spoke the number. "Six."

They didn't know he was stopping at the Astor. They did know he visited the bar. Gordon couldn't have been there by accident. Someone wiser than he had suggested this particular bar. Someone, a pale lavender girl, two young men cut from a stereotyped pattern? And a slinking shadow frightened to death.

Piers left the elevator without good night. His room, front and center, was near. He opened his door, locked it after him. He didn't make a light, the lights of Broadway shone gaudily. As they shadowed, he crossed to the windows, opened them wide to the sound and the brightness of maelstrom below.

He stood, a frail reed, between this light and the darkness. He would not be eliminated. Not by a ratlike man with a scant yellow beard, not by the experts of European intrigue. Nor, he smiled, by the ambitions of Gordon and his sure, steady perfection. De Witt Gordon to succeed the Secretary? No. It must be he, Piers Hunt.

He alone knew where the Secretary was. He alone knew the two unmarked graves in the African sand. Gordon was eaten with anxiety. Piers knew that Secretary Anstruther was dead.

II

Piers had the morning papers sent to his room with breakfast. They were featuring the imminent International Peace Conclave as if nothing untoward had happened. Perhaps the secret had been kept; perhaps the press didn't know that Anstruther was missing.

Brecklein had arrived and—his nostrils narrowed —the dirty Schern. That arrogant sentimentalist, Dessaye, was here. The French again would toady to the stronger nations. Once France had been a strong nation. That was before his time, a part of history. She would assuage her fears anew with another loan. Lord Evanhurst arrived today; with him Watkins. Piers could count on Watkins, but Watkins, like himself, was only an undersecretary. Evanhurst was believed to be one of the chief proponents of the withdrawal.

The Dominions were against it but they wouldn't fight the mother country, not if she were lined up with the United States. He didn't know about the Russians. China would vote with the States; South America with the majority. South Africa was for withdrawal; they were too far away to fear, and there was

17

German blood. North Africa would follow Britain. As for Equatorial Africa, Black Africa, the important new province—it was an unknown quantity. It would go as Fabian willed. And Fabian's will was more unknown than the territory he represented. Piers feared its expression.

He searched the papers for news of Fabian but there was none. Perhaps the New York reporters didn't know the importance of the Secretary of Equatorial Africa. Few of the conference did. If he could get to Fabian, talk with him, person to person, he might possibly make him see, understand. Fabian might well hold the balance of power in the voting. Most of Asia, even Asia Minor, would listen to what Fabian had to say. It was possible that South America would be swayed by him; there had been portents in regional meetings that the mass of the people of South America considered themselves allied with the dark continent.

If he could find Fabian he could at least learn his reactions to the border incidents. He could demand an explanation of the telegram and its aftermath. He would know from the answer or the evasion if Brecklein had got to the African leader first.

The most important thing now was that he himself not die. Last night had proved he wasn't safe. The man who had followed him hadn't been the killer but he had been the first messenger from Death. Piers wasn't certain why he was being hunted. The most valid reason was because of his determination to block the withdrawal of the international military from Germany. But no one had knowledge of that.

There were a few, yes, Watkins, Nickerson, Abrahm-sky, Australia's Sandys, the young Czech delegate, all undersecretaries, all unimportant, who knew his convictions. But they knew as well—or thought they did—his inability to act on these. They believed his hands were tied as were their own.

It was improbable that this was the reason behind his being followed. The more unimportant causes were the more probable. Conceivably some of the schemers might believe that the Secretary of Peace was purposely remaining out of sight until the opening of the conclave in order that he might face it without the insinuating propaganda of the various legations. Granting this premise, Piers could be followed to lead to Secretary Anstruther's place of retirement. This premise did not carry the threat of death.

But this one did: If the intriguers knew that the Secretary would not appear a *Deus ex machina* at the opening of the conclave, it could be believed that Piers carried his final instructions. Careful as he had been, it could be known that he had the Secretary's papers. If certain nations did not wish these voiced, and they did not, Piers would need to be eliminated. This theory carried promise of sudden death, death within five days' time.

He didn't want to die. This was his world. He liked work, fair fight, and the blue hills of adventure. He liked the stimulus of books. He liked long thoughts, and man, and some men. He liked earth in its greenness and in its barrenness; he liked the machine and the elements and the stars. Like was a poor word for it. Life was of him. It was he. He savored it and he gulped it. He didn't want to die until he had been filled to saturation.

He had spent four years during the Last War, that Second World War, in daily combat with death. He hadn't wanted to die then but he hadn't been afraid. Now he was afraid to die. The fear had nothing to do with fear of losing his identity. He didn't believe in oblivion. Death would be the new adventure. Nor had his fear to do with giving up this life. That brought resentment but not fear. He feared because if he died there was no one to fight for peace. There were multitudes who wanted peace, who blossomed in the peace of these past twelve years, who clung to the promise of everlasting peace. There were many who had forgotten war and some who had never known it, who believed therefore that peace was inevitable. Even Watkins and Sandys could not fight for peace. It wasn't that they lacked courage or will; it was that they were not yet appointed. His was the appointment.

He stood from the bed and crumpled the papers. Anstruther's death should not be without purpose. The old man had been good; he had had the simplicity of goodness. This was not enough when the apes stirred man to bestiality again. The good could not stop the depredation. Only man who had risen from brute man, who recognized the evil gropings, could do that. Piers could and would do it. He was not traveling to Samarra this season.

He crossed to the window and stood there, unseen, looking down at Broadway below. Morning Broadway was a different street from that of night. It was

almost quiet now; there were few walkers; the policeman at the intersection was unharried. The police
force was for the protection of honest citizens. What
would the Commissioner do if Broadway demanded
the police be removed from its environs? The idea
was too ludicrous for consideration. The same idea
for a different street should be laughed out of the
peace conclave. It wouldn't be.

He wished he knew where to find Fabian. A plane
whirred overhead. No one below looked up, no one
burrowed for shelter, the old Broadway trolley continued to bump along the tracks, the leisurely spring
morning was unchanged. That was peace. There was
a time when the sound of a plane had brought the
terrible silence of fear.

He stretched his lean body and went towards the
shower. He wasn't going to die. It would help, however, if he knew for certain who wanted him to die.
It could be Gordon. Gordon intended to step into the
old man's shoes. He had directed his career carefully
towards that achievement. But Gordon didn't know
that Anstruther was dead. Only Piers knew that. And
it would never occur to Gordon that Piers might be a
contender for the post.

It must be Brecklein. Brecklein knew or sensed
something. The exquisite German espionage system
wouldn't be blotted out by twelve or twice twelve
years. It would if anything be more perceptive by its
enforced quiet. The presence of Schern as an envoy of
appeal to the court wasn't by accident. Schern had
been the key man in their intelligence during the
Last War. The inner key. Piers knew that well.

He scrubbed himself happily. He wasn't afraid of Brecklein or of his associates. He knew exactly how their minds would function; the traveling salesman was an example. He needn't be afraid of quick death at their hands. Theirs would not be a shot in the dark; their passion to know would insist that they first probe his motives and intentions.

And now he wasn't afraid of failure either. The depression he'd brought home with him last night from Washington, result of a day of lethargy and of being shunted from one minor bureaucrat to another, had lifted. He didn't like the prospect of the inactive days ahead—the conclave would not open until Sunday, four days to wait—but it was an essential part of the plan. To remain in the background, to wait, until the time was ripe for striking. He could wait.

The phone rang as he was brushing his dust-colored hair. He scowled. There was no reason for it to ring. No one knew a Mr. Pierce stopping at the Astor. No one but the clerk could call. Reflectively Piers moved to answer but his hand remained pressed down on the instrument. He turned away, finished dressing to the punctuation of its ringing. It had stopped before he left the room.

He didn't take his room key to the desk. The night clerk had put a name to him last night; it was possible the day clerk also would recognize him. Later he would inquire, after the seeker, if there were one, had gone. He went out the side door onto 45th street. He walked over to Broadway, stood for a moment in the doorway of the Walgreen's drugstore on the corner. On impulse he cut into the street up to the traffic officer. He waited until the patrolman blew his whistle and lifted his white gloved hand for traffic change.

Piers stood equal in height if not in breadth to the officer. Assignment in Africa had worn him thin. He asked with the right careless curiosity, "Hear about the accident up the street last night?"

"Yeah. I wasn't on duty." He continued manipulating traffic as he spoke. "Did you witness it?"

"Not exactly. Not till it was over." Piers spoke with clear conscience and candid eyes. "Had my back to it. Who was the fellow?"

"Don't know. If you were there last night you ought to report in to the Precinct. It's the Eighteenth, up on Fifty-fourth street. Captain Devlin is trying to round up all the witnesses."

"He must have been someone important," Piers said carelessly. "But I didn't see anything in the papers."

The policeman held traffic for two women and a little girl with dyed yellow curls and white tassels topping her boots. One of the women examined Piers. When they reached the curb, the cop blew his whistle. "Wasn't that. Only some of the witnesses say the guy was being chased. Some of them say he was pushed."

"Sorry I can't help out. I was just too late." Piers moved on, lounging across to the east side of Broadway.

The officer didn't look after him. Doubtless took him for one of the unemployed actors who emerged at the late morning hour. The officer hadn't been suspicious.

There was risk in it but he wanted to visit the precinct where the accident had been reported. Wisely he had changed to protective coloring today. The sand-brown gabardine, the panama, wouldn't fit a description of a dark suit and hat. No spectator could have described his face; it was any face, thin, tanned, no distinguishing marks.

He walked on uptown. It was worth the chance for the possibility of finding out the fellow's name. A lost article. A briefcase. Lost in the excitement over the accident. A good enough excuse. He strode north the nine blocks, turned west on 54th, to the severe gray stone of number 306. He didn't hesitate at the door; he pushed in.

The sergeant at the desk was big and red. A tuft of saffron gray hair grew over each ear. He sucked his pen and exhaled, "What's yours?"

Piers stated without preamble, "I lost my briefcase last night. By any chance has it been turned in here?"

The sergeant had a list of questions, routine for lost and found.

Piers avoided name and address, describing, "Alligator, brown. Papers in it."

"What kind of papers?"

He smiled, deciding to hold his imagination to a guise which would fit. "Plays. Manuscript plays, that is."

The sergeant's nose didn't consider that of much importance.

"It was a good briefcase," Piers insisted. "Good alligator." A good alligator is a dead alligator. He continued answering the queries. "It was somewhere in the Paramount block. I think it must have been knocked from my hand when the accident occurred."

When he spoke the word "accident" the watery blue eyes with the yellowed pupils, the disinterested eyes, suddenly became crisp as china.

"You mean the accident—you mean the guy that jumped in front of a taxi?"

"Fell or jumped or was pushed," Piers said. He said it blithely, as if he'd taken part in a sidewalk session after its occurrence.

"You want to see Captain Devlin," the sergeant nodded. He got to his feet as if they pained him and he padded to an inner door.

Piers let his voice follow eagerly. "Does he know about my briefcase?" He lighted a cigarette after the officer disappeared. This was better than he had expected, a first-hand talk with the captain. He wasn't apprehensive; he couldn't be connected with the accident; he had not come here to speak of it but to inquire for lost property. He was curious as to whether the police had discovered the dead man to be important or whether this was normal procedure for the many like accidents which must occur in the city. If the latter, the police were to be respected for their careful regard for death.

The old sergeant stuck his head through the door. "You, there. Come on in. Captain says he wants to see you."

"Certainly."

Piers followed the man down a corridor into a drab box of a room. It was furnished with a too large desk, an old wooden bench and chair, a calendar portraying an Indian girl stepping into a birch canoe, and a large brass cuspidor. The man behind the desk was large, gray-haired, ruddy-faced. He wore his hat on the back of his head.

"I'm Captain Devlin. Sit down, Mister . . . Sit down, O'Leary."

The sergeant sat on the chair. Piers lounged easily on the old bench.

"Your name?" Captain Devlin asked. He had a green pencil with a large brass clip on it pointed at a paper. His desk was assorted with papers.

"George Henderson." Piers didn't hesitate. He'd been Thompson in Washington, he was Pierce at the Astor, but Henderson came easily to his lips. He knew these names well, always he used ordinary names, nothing too common or too unusual to attract suspicion. "I lost my briefcase—it's of brown alligator."

"Yeah," Captain Devlin interrupted. "Your address, Mr. Henderson?"

They couldn't be meaning to detain him while they checked on this. He was a casual. An innocent bystander. He said as if he were slightly ashamed of it, "It's seventeen Sheridan Square." He had been born at 17 Sheridan Square. He hoped the building still stood. "I'm staying with friends there—it's just temporary. I expect to get a place of my own soon. I'm a playwright." He gave the captain a smile both proud and happy, and then he frowned a little. "My newest manuscripts are in that briefcase and it's very important I find it. Of course I have my rough drafts but I don't want to have to type the whole thing again —" He prattled, at ease in his role.

The captain interrupted again. "You witnessed the accident in front of the Paramount last night?"

"But I didn't. I was right there but I was walking the other way." He said with slight regret, "I just missed it."

The captain's square face took on a shade of disappointment. "You don't know if he fell or was pushed then?"

"No," Piers said. "No, I don't. I'm sorry. I heard the brakes of the taxi when it stopped. Everyone was terribly excited, all talking at once. Some said the man jumped and some said he was pushed. I couldn't wait though. I was late for an appointment. It wasn't until I was in the theater later that I missed my brief case. It's been turned in?"

The sergeant said, "No. Nothing good ever is."

Piers was emphatic. "It was a good briefcase. I'd hate to lose it. It means so much work——" This time he did the breaking off and his eyes were bright with curiosity. "Who was the man who was killed? Was he someone important? Is that why you think he was pushed?"

Captain Devlin shook his head. "We don't think he was pushed. But some of the witnesses say he was. There's always witnesses with big imaginations in any accident case——"

Piers waited, taut. He couldn't repeat his question. He mustn't be anything but a naïve young playwright in this room. He could play the role. His face was unlined, boyish enough for his thirty-six years. He waited and the identity was forthcoming.

"He wasn't anyone at all," Devlin continued. "John Smith."

"John Smith," Piers repeated, and then he brightened to hide his disappointment. "That's like a play, Captain. That anyone should actually be named John Smith and be in an accident."

"It was his name." Devlin tapped his pencil. "He was identified late last night. By his uncle. We could write it off as closed if it weren't for those two damn witnesses insisting he was pushed."

Piers said thoughtfully as if weaving a plot, "And of course that means the uncle will press you—"

"He doesn't give a damn. He doesn't think the guy was pushed." Devlin was grim. "It's the Commissioner. He don't like loose ends." He seemed to see Piers again. "Well, young man, if your briefcase turns up, we'll notify you." It was dismissal.

Piers said, "Thank you, sir. And I'm really sorry I didn't witness your accident." He followed the sergeant back into the outer room.

"John Smith," he said. "It's funny—a real John Smith."

The sergeant gruffed, "He musta changed it from Schmidt. The old man could hardly talk English."

Piers moved, reluctant, into the spring sunshine.

2.

Leaving the precinct station, he seemed to be leaving safety behind. He felt an impulse to turn back, to tell the dull and honest sergeant, the worried and rigid captain, "I am in danger. Will you give me protection before I lie beside John Smith?"

He could not. Where would he get accusing Brecklein, the accredited German envoy to the Peace Conclave? He would be dismissed as a crank, or worse, he would be detained for observation. He had no proof to offer. That the final comment of the old sergeant was for him proof sufficient that the Germans were after him did not mean that he was without understanding of the nebulous quality of this proof for others. But it was, for him, sufficient.

He would have liked to inquire further, to have elicited a description of the uncle. Possibly he could have done so out of idle curiosity but in retrospect it might have awakened suspicion. As much as he would welcome police protection, he could not afford to become the object of police suspicion. Nor was he credulous enough to believe that the police would have difficulty in finding him again if they set out with that purpose. Manhattan was a small island. His hope was that he would escape attention, that there would be no reason for them to seek one George Henderson.

He walked back to Broadway. It would be wise to call Gordon before the man called him. The time was near noon. He stopped at a drugstore, looked up the number of the New York branch of the Peace Department. Normally the branch office wasn't important but with the Conclave at hand Gordon would make his headquarters there. Anstruther and the first Peace delegates had been wise in their determination that conclaves should not be held in political capitals. The United States Halls of Peace stood on the banks of the Hudson, not on the Potomac.

He dropped the coin, dialed. Three times he gave his name, Piers alone, waiting permission to speak to the important Gordon. One voice actually spoke of Secretary Gordon. Piers' mouth twisted. Gordon knew how to erect a structure.

He was eventually put through to the rich assurance of that voice. It was impossible to believe in the dark burrows of danger and death when *Hind* Gordon spoke. "Piers? The girl said Mr. Pierce and I couldn't place it. I rang you but the hotel desk said you weren't there."

"I went out early," Piers evaded. "Any word from the Secretary?"

The warm cadence was troubled. "No. I don't know what to think." He broke off. "Lunch with me, Piers. I'll cancel my appointments. It's important we decide what we're to do."

"To do?" Piers asked softly.

"Yes. If he—" He broke off. "Can you lunch with me, Piers?"

"Yes."

"Make it the Chatham at one. It's secluded, we can talk without disturbance."

Piers rang off. The slant smile remained on his face as he left the booth. Gordon was disturbed. It was good that Gordon be disturbed. As long as he could be kept in that state he wouldn't be able to move swiftly, without deviation, to the coveted goal.

Piers decided against returning to the hotel. Whoever had rung his room might be waiting his appearance. If possible he would delay until the cocktail or dinner hour, until the lobby was well filled. He wanted no trouble. He didn't believe the call could be any more than a clerk's inquiry; yet . . . Yet until last night he hadn't believed it was known to anyone that he was in New York.

He walked out again into the crowded noon. He covered leisurely the path between the towering flanks of Rockefeller Center to Fifth. The shop windows on the way were summer bright; tulips bloomed in the gardens. He lingered in their color. As he moved, a shadow seemed to move with him.

It could be he was overly alert. He had thought some paces back, at the haberdasher's down the street, that a shadow loitered. He moved on Fifth, still leisurely, with curiosity, no fear. There was nothing to fear at high noon in this not only crowded but highly civilized sector of the avenue. He could be curious. If he were followed, he would like to know if it stemmed from the hotel or the precinct house. The latter was more probable. John Smith hadn't completed his assignment last night. But John Smith's uncle, or the-friends-of-my-uncle, might well be watching who would call at the station. It was undeniable that members of Brecklein's party would recognize Piers Hunt. Brecklein wouldn't leave that to chance.

He walked slowly down Fifth, allowing the swift tempo of the street to stream past him. It would be next to impossible to surprise a follower in the crowd. It was momentarily unimportant. He could make certain he was not trailed before returning to the Astor.

DOROTHY B. HUGHES

He reached the Chatham slightly before one o'clock, left his hat with the quiet elderly man at the hatstand, and waited in the red velvet foyer. It was cool, empty. The hushed room beyond had but a few diners; the waiters wore the masks of old retainers.

Gordon came at one-ten. He said, "Glad you could make it, Piers," and, "Good afternoon, Bronson," as if the checkman were a private club employee. His handshake was that of an important man.

"I hadn't anything else to do," Piers said with amusement. "I haven't any friends to look up. My grandmother—last of the family—died years ago. I've been away too long."

Gordon led into the dining room. He nodded to none of the other diners. Each waiter they passed spoke, "Good day, Mr. Gordon." To the maître d'hôtel he said, "If we could have the corner spot, Jules?"

"Certainement, Mr. Gordon."

It was secluded enough, a rounded couch that commanded the room, behind it walls alone. There could be no eavesdropping.

"You'll have a Martini? Very dry for me, Jules." He was a good host, as if born to the purple. He suggested the whitefish with a superb sauce, pale wine, a mixed salad. Piers deferred to his taste.

"Not hearty," Gordon apologized. "Too hot today."

He was filled with anxiety. The cool gray of his suit, his healthy face, his manners, couldn't hide it. He spoke over the cocktail, "I don't know what's happened. What can have happened, Piers?"

32

Piers watched him over the rim of his glass. "Perhaps he stopped off in South America."

"No. That's what I've told the President and the Secretary of State, but no. Not unless he told you—" He waited.

"He didn't plan any stopover," Piers said with finality. "None he mentioned."

Gordon worried it. "There's been no plane accident reported. What can have happened?"

Piers said, "Perhaps it's a disappearance."

Gordon looked quickly.

"There have been cases. Planes disappearing. Never heard of thereafter. No one knows."

"That's weird." Gordon smiled, but his smile wasn't sure.

"Weird but possible," Piers said. *"There are more things in heaven and earth, Horatio, than are dreamt of . . . "*

"No." Gordon rejected. "I don't believe that."

"What do you believe?" Piers asked softly.

"I don't know. I tell you I don't know." He broke off while the lunch was served, continued again, "He's long overdue. A week and no word. You saw him off?"

"On Monday. A week ago Monday."

"When did you arrive here?"

"Friday last."

Gordon laid down his fork. "Friday? You've been here that long? What have you been doing? Why didn't you let me know?"

Piers took his time in answering. "I needed a rest." He smiled. "I knew you'd put me to work if I showed up, Gordon."

Gordon shook his head.

"I had a vacation due. You don't know how fatiguing field work can be. Particularly just before a conclave."

"You didn't know the old man wasn't here?"

Piers shrugged. "Not until I went to Washington yesterday did I even suspect." His brows went up. "Then I did suspect. Those clerks in the Peace Department don't hide things well, Gordon. I daresay Washington's seething with rumors."

"Rumors can't hurt us," Gordon replied with certainty. "The worst they can say is that he's sick—a collapse. Rumors won't go beyond that." He scowled. "What I'm afraid of is fact. When the fact that he's missing becomes known—as it must by Sunday—what then?"

"You're afraid the Conclave will fall to pieces?"

"Yes—no, that can't happen, Piers. Biennial meetings. Members convening from all over the globe— do you know we're to have almost full representation this time? It can't collapse. But without him to hold it steady—already there's so much of little bickering —cartels—cliques— It's an important meeting, Piers."

"Yes," Piers said.

Gordon leaned across the table. "I believe it is paramount we let no one know in advance that the old man may not be present."

"Yes," Piers said.

"If that were known, I don't know what feuds might flare up. He's always kept them down. He's believed in International Peace."

"Yes," Piers said again. He touched his napkin to his mouth. "Yes. You've hit it, Gordon." He looked at him for a moment almost with envy. "That belief of Anstruther's and a few others has kept the peace this far. That belief must go on. If the believers can keep it flaming, the way he did, if they can hold it long enough we'll breed out war. But you must have men who have as passionate a belief in peace as once certain men had in war."

Gordon said slowly, "It isn't war I'm afraid of. If you keep the nations prospering they're content. No need for war. And when there isn't a need for an element, it disappears."

"If you aren't afraid of war, then what?" He asked it quietly.

Gordon touched his well-groomed mustache. He said, "I want our country to maintain its place as the leader in International Peace."

"A nationalist," Piers smiled. Gordon might well have said: I want to be as important as Anstruther has been. I want to hold that most important cabinet post, Secretary of Peace of the United States; I want the post to continue as it has for the decade of Anstruther's secretaryship, to be hereditary president of the Conclave.

Gordon reddened, defending himself, "Maybe, Piers. But I can't help thinking our country's pretty important. If you'd been in my place in Washington these years— We've made this Peace thing. We've forced it to work. I don't want to see our place threatened if Anstruther is—if anything's happened to the old man."

Piers took his tea scalding, plain. "I don't think it's important who stands for what in the Conclave, what position any nation holds, as long as all stand for peace."

"An internationalist." Gordon smiled now.

"Perhaps. Perhaps it's just that peace is important to me, more important than any man"—he finished the tea—"or any nation."

Gordon bit his lip. "We haven't decided what to do. It's up to us to carry things along until Anstruther —at least until the Conclave is in session. You'll help out?"

Piers didn't commit himself. He asked rather, "How did you know I was here, Gordon? There's no use saying that meeting at the Astor was opportune."

Gordon flushed and then he laughed. "I'd been looking for you. Nickerson cabled you were coming."

Not Nickerson. Wiles, perhaps, but not Nickerson. Piers had definitely stated that this was a Z-13 mission; that meant utter secrecy. Gordon didn't know that.

"I sent a cable to you—Z code—about the whereabouts of Anstruther. Nickerson replied that you were in this country."

Possibly. But not Nickerson. He wouldn't make mistakes.

"And the Astor?" Piers' eyes smiled.

"I'd tried all the hotels. You're not under your name?"

"No," Piers admitted.

"I remembered that evening in Berne—three years

ago, wasn't it? Your weltschmerz for New York, in particular Broadway and the Astor."

Piers said, "Good deducing. I might use you on a mission some day."

Gordon lettered the check. He looked up from it to Piers' face. "Just why did you come to New York at this time?"

"To attend the Conclave." He pushed back from the table. "I've been determined for a long time to attend this particular conclave, Gordon."

3.

They recovered their hats, stood for a moment at the door. Gordon said, "I wish you'd bring your papers around to the office, Piers. Perhaps if we went over what you have we might find a hint."

"I don't have papers."

Gordon didn't believe him. "Your reports?"

"I take notes in my head. Dictate from memory. The girls in the Berne office make it readable."

It was inconceivable to Gordon, Gordon of the great mahogany desk in Washington, the disciplined files. Gordon of the private office in the Park Avenue branch of the Peace Department, more desks, more files.

"Reports aren't my job, Gordon. Thank God, I ought to say. It's the human equation I contend with, the subterfuge, the unexpressed yearnings, the crosscurrents. It comes out all right in the end."

They stood on the corner of Park.

"I'll look over your papers if you like," he suggested.

"You needn't," Gordon said abruptly. "Don't think I haven't been over and over them, particularly the reports the old man sent on this trip. Although they were brief, inconclusive. I don't know why you needed him in Africa. If he hadn't gone there— Those little border troubles—"

Those little border troubles, incidents, had been too carefully brewed. Piers had needed Secretary Anstruther. If the Secretary saw for himself, he would, despite Evanhurst, refuse Germany's request. He would sway the Conclave to his belief. Piers was silent now.

Gordon said, "I must get back to the office. By the way, I want you to come along with me tomorrow night. A small dinner Lord Evanhurst is giving."

Piers shook his head. "I'll help you out, Gordon, but not in the social swim. You'll have to handle that yourself. I've been in the bush too long."

"Nonsense," Gordon jeered. His eyes turned somber. "Besides it isn't merely social. It's for some of the envoys. A gesture of good will, peace."

"Will Fabian be there?" He forgot to be cautious.

"Fabian?"

"Equatorial Africa."

"I know," Gordon said impatiently. "But you know he doesn't ever appear. Fancies himself sort of a black monk, for all I hear. Even so this will be only major powers. A small dinner." He laid his hand on Piers' arm. "I think you should be present, Piers. I'll handle the social side but there'll be plenty of observing for you. He's having the German group. Purposely."

Piers accepted. "I'll come. I'll be delighted to come." His mouth narrowed. "I want to meet Brecklein."

"You haven't?"

"Somehow I've missed that. I've even missed Schern. By the skin of my teeth, I might add, during the Last War."

Gordon said, "That's right, you were in Intelligence, weren't you?"

"Part of the time." He turned. "Thanks for lunch. Tomorrow night then."

"Sevenish. I'll pick you up."

"I'll probably be out. I don't like hotel rooms. Where can I meet you?"

"I'm at the Waldorf," Gordon said with hidden pride. He hesitated. "I didn't see any report of your dead man in the papers. Did you learn any details?"

"Only his name," Piers said. "Johann Schmidt." His eyes remained candid on Gordon's as he spoke. There was no flicker of surprise or understanding visible. But brown eyes were opaque. They could hide what lighter pigments gave away.

He knew he was followed now. He stopped for a shoeshine. He bought a dress tie for which he had no use. He leaned against a Schrafft's counter for limeade. He dallied at shop windows. Each time when he stopped, each time he set out, the same shadow dogged his steps. He was beginning to fill out the outline, a burly man, tall, in a dark shapeless suit, a shapeless fedora pulled not too far over his eyes. A chain, glinting in the sun, across a protruding vest. Some kind of charm dangling from it. Feet that walked heavily, the way the old sergeant's had walked, as if they'd been used too long. This follower was not sly as last night's had been. Nor inept. This man no matter how the game was played would follow, without imagination, under orders.

He must be eliminated before Piers turned back towards the Astor. Piers had nothing to do with his time. All that was necessary had been accomplished before he left Africa. His game now was a waiting one only. He could lead this heavy man as far as he desired. He followed Fifth Avenue as it led, the crowds growing more thin and more rich as he entered the upper Fifties. He turned left at 59th and headed for the Plaza. He passed the weathered stone fountain, entered the dignified portals.

Within the cool somberness of the lobby, he moved slowly, waiting to see if the man behind him would enter. He didn't wait long. The bulk bought a newspaper and sat down in one of the old velvet chairs. The newspaper hid the sagging jowls, not the eyes. Under the hat brim these watched without seeming to watch.

Piers walked to the desk. He said, "I am Piers Hunt." The clerk hadn't been here long enough to be worn to the rich patina of the hotel. He hadn't been here long enough to remember the young boy who had lived with his grandmother in that sky suite overlooking the park. Cornelia Piers who had died after Munich, before Dunquerque. This empty man didn't know that the dark wood, the jeweled velvets were the nostalgia of home to Piers Hunt. He couldn't know how the scent of velvet and polished wood had remained with Piers through blood and flame and thunder, and after, through the years of labor for peace.

Piers said it, "I am Piers Hunt," and he smiled a little when the clerk's impassive face expressed only impassivity. He said, "I should like a room here." He made the arrangements, paying a week in advance. "My luggage will be around later. Will you arrange to have it unpacked, if you please?" He took the key, refusing to go up to the room. It would hold little resemblance to the exquisite tower where Cornelia Piers had lived and died. He signed the registration card, giving Berne as his address, his back a screen to the man in the chair near the entrance.

He would send a couple of bags around sometime today, order them and their contents from Abercrombie. He had no intention of using this room; it was no more than a number which Gordon could call. He would ring Gordon in the morning to report he had now registered under his own name. He smiled again realizing how much more acceptable a Piers Hunt at the Plaza would be to Gordon than one at the Astor. Without import as it seemed, Gordon's snobbery had been of undeniable value to the man and to the cementing of his position in Washington. He wouldn't call it snobbery; it would be the right thing, white, as against the wrong, black. One who acted from innate instincts alone could not conceive the importance these niceties assumed to men whose consciousness of the right thing was born out of study and decision, who had to fight to grasp the consciousness. Only those things for which a man could or would fight had any real importance. One must fight, or stand ready to fight, even for peace.

Piers walked to the doors, passing the newspaper and the chair. He paused long enough to observe the faint reflection of the man in the glass. He was folding the paper, watching Piers where he stood. Piers left the hotel. It was almost four o'clock, time to throw off the tracker if he was to see about Plaza luggage before returning to the Astor.

But once outside in the warm spring he was reluctant to return to shop windows. The park lay at hand; greenness of earth offered a respite from violence and unknown fear. He followed the winding path, moving into spring and forgetfulness. There was scent of budding tree, of grass roots pushing from the deeps of soil to sun and color. Children played on the slopes, their voices calling out in the very joy of sound and movement. There were lovers, two by two, silent in their joy and as heedless of their insecurity as were the children. The young, the old, those passing from young to old, none knew how false was their blithe acceptance of these peaceful hours. None knew that even now, in this very city, there were men plotting to threaten their peace, to plunge the world again into destruction and death. If they were told— if he stopped before that young mother to say, "There are in this city men who wish to tear your little son with molten iron. At this moment men are plotting to pump this spring air full of searing gas"—she would think him insane. She would commend him to the towering blue policeman up the path. Memory was that fleeting.

He sat down on the bench, took off his hat in order that the small wind might cool his burning head. Anger, the anger that flooded him whenever he thought of any man daring to threaten the continuation of peace, was no weapon. The weapons he should use were the weapons Gordon would employ, careful consideration of incidents, the right relationship with the right men, cerebral action, not that of spirit. Gordon could help him. Piers didn't know why he was afraid to approach his associate when he needed help as badly as he did. He didn't know for certain that Gordon was pledged to the viewpoint of Lord Evanhurst, that Gordon had been influenced without knowing it by the wily Schern or convinced by Brecklein's weight. All he had for basis of his belief was that brief discussion with Anstruther the night before the old man was to return to Washington. Anstruther had said of his own convictions, "I don't know. I don't know what is the right thing." Anstruther's own belief in peace was too profound to believe that any nation would threaten it. And Anstruther had said, "I believe Gordon thinks we should withdraw."

Even if that was Gordon's opinion, Piers should have confidence in his own power to change it. Why then did he hesitate to speak? He didn't like Gordon, had never liked him, but Gordon wouldn't hesitate to use someone with whom he was not in sympathy to gain desired ends. That was why Gordon had importance.

He was afraid of Gordon's help. Because Gordon in his youth was wise in the ancient ways of ape diplomacy. He must play it lone, knowing there was a small nucleus who would stand with him if he were allowed to speak.

He saw the burly man then, seated on the bench below him taking his ease. He didn't like that man; he didn't like the damp shapelessness of the oversized suit; he didn't like the slack face and the peering eyes. He didn't like being followed. It was time to do something about it.

The policeman was still there on the path, a young, strong guardian of the inherent rights of innocent man. Piers walked to him. The policeman turned a helpful face. Piers said, "That man—on the bench there—is following me. He's followed me all afternoon. I don't like being followed."

The policeman's face waded with doubt, alert doubt. Another crackpot, it said.

Piers insisted. "You don't believe me. I'm going to leave the park now. I'll walk past him. You watch. He'll follow."

"Why's he following you?" A doubt had entered the officer's doubt.

"I don't know. You might ask him. And tell him please that I don't like being followed. If he doesn't stop, I'm going to do something about it."

He moved leisurely, past the bench where the heavy man sat waiting. He was only a few paces past when he heard the altercation, heard the abused rumble, "Do I got to get a cop's permission to leave Central Park when I wanta?"

Piers didn't look back. He moved rapidly and he caught a cab just before reaching the mouth of the entrance. He rode to Abercrombie's. No cab followed. He selected a large suitcase and a small one, good expensive leather; gave a list of shirts, socks, underwear, sleeping array, enough to fill the bags. He included toilet articles, everything necessary. He would present the luggage to Gordon when this was all over. He paid, gave his name and address, The Plaza, asked that they be sent around tomorrow. For reason of the outfitting, lest the clerk be suspicious and check with the hotel, he mentioned luggage overdue from the continent.

His spirits were light when he went back out on Madison. His trailer was lost; he was respectably housed for Gordon's curiosity without losing his necessary anonymity. He took a cab to the Astor. The lobby was humming with conversation piece and the music of the cocktail hour. An iced drink before going to his room for a shower and change. There was no reason to hurry. He could dine when he pleased, go around later to a theater.

The bar was crowded. He took his place at the far end and ordered a daiquiri. He saw the lavender-haired girl as he waited. She was moving between the tables, hatless, in some sort of lavender afternoon dress. Her eyes were on Piers.

He sipped from the small cold glass and watched her. He was slightly disturbed when he realized she was moving to him. He stood waiting, still watching her until she was directly in front of him. He saw then, his eyes accustomed to the distortion of light, that her hair was flaxen and her dress white. He saw that she was very young.

Her voice was quiet. "Where is my father?"

Something changed in his eyes. It happened too quickly for him to be on guard. He said, "I believe you've mistaken me for someone."

She said, "I am Bianca Anstruther," and he didn't speak. He didn't move his eyes from her small graven face. She repeated, "Where is my father?"

He answered then. "I don't know."

He noticed her hands, the fingers clenched to paleness.

She said, "You were the last person to see my father. Witt told me last night. You say you put him aboard the plane."

Witt must be Gordon. DeWitt Gordon.

Piers said, "I put him on the plane, yes. I don't know where he is." In heaven or hell or the place where lost souls linger.

"Where is he?"

He asked gravely, "Will you join me in a drink, Miss Anstruther? There's a table. I'd like to talk with you."

She said, "I'm with friends. There's no need to talk. Simply answer my question—"

"I believe there is. If you can spare me a few moments."

She glanced over her shoulder and his eyes followed. He saw the table. A round white hat, lavender now, marked her place. There was a young man, perhaps one of those who had been with her last night. And there was Hugo von Eynar.

For the moment he was stone, not breathing, not stirring. He hadn't expected von Eynar. And yet he should have known. Now it was complete, the trinity. Brecklein to weigh with the financiers, Schern to scheme with the politicians; von Eynar, the slender golden aristocrat, to charm the recalcitrant. For a moment—only for that—he regretted the imposing of this appointment on himself. He regretted it while his eyes searched for the one who must be there with Hugo but who was not. Yet he knew even in that moment that if his eyes should find her, it could make no difference. It must not.

He moved again. "Do your friends know what you came to ask me?"

She shook her head slightly. "I said I wished to speak to an old friend."

He took her arm then and moved her to a table. He stopped a waiter, asked, "Miss Anstruther?"

She shook her head.

"Two daiquiris." He demanded of her, "Do you realize how carefully Gordon is guarding the secret of your father's absence?"

She was scornful. "Certainly."

"And why no one must know?"

Scorn continued to twist her mouth. "I understand how important my father's work is. I've grown up under its importance. Do you think I would do anything to jeopardize it?" Her eyes burned into his. "But I want to know where he is."

He answered slowly. "I would like to tell you. Believe me, I would like to tell you."

"He left in a private plane?"

"Yes."

"Who was with him?"

"He was alone. That wasn't unusual, Miss Anstruther. You should know that. He flew all over the five continents alone."

"He was to transfer in Lisbon to the Clipper?"

"Yes."

"He never reached Lisbon."

Piers said evenly, "No, he never reached Lisbon."

The waiter set the frosted glasses. Piers said, "I'm not your enemy. You needn't be afraid to drink with me."

She lifted the glass by its thin stem. "I'm not afraid," she said. "Not of you." She drank and she asked, "What did you do after he left Alexandria?"

"I flew to Berne. My orders."

"When? That same day?"

He spoke with care. "I had two days' work before I could get away."

There was pleading in her throat. "And you heard nothing? No report of a missing plane?"

"There was no report." He spoke with finality.

She sipped again. "Who was his pilot?"

"As I told Gordon last night, I had never seen the pilot before."

She seized avidly on this. "But that wasn't usual. He never flew with a pilot unknown to him."

"I know. But I didn't know at the time that the pilot was unknown to Secretary Anstruther. I don't know that yet. However, after the Secretary had taken off, when I realized I did not know the pilot, I made inquiries as to who he was."

48

"Then you sensed something was wrong?"

"Perhaps," he admitted.

"Who was he—the pilot?"

"A German, Gundar Abersohn, with a good flying record. He'd been in the Luftwaffe during the Last War."

She finished her cocktail and the glass trembled as she set it down. She said, "I think he's dead."

Piers was silent.

"Witt thinks he's dead. He won't say it, but he thinks so."

"He is disturbed," Piers admitted.

"What do you think?" she demanded suddenly.

Piers spread his hands. "I don't know. I don't think. But as I suggested to Witt, there have been plane disappearances before now."

"An accident. But there are always traces."

"Not always. And I don't even mean that. I mean disappearance without traces."

She shivered. "That isn't normal."

"No, it isn't. Nor is your father's disappearance normal."

She insisted, "You think he's dead too."

"I wouldn't say it," he said. "Gordon won't say it. You should be careful not to let anyone read your thoughts. It could do untold harm. Anyone."

She said, "I'm careful. I'm always careful. I told you that."

Not careful in her friends, however. What was she doing in the company of Hugo von Eynar? How had she met him? Through Gordon, perhaps. That could mean that Gordon was definitely committed to act

49

with Evanhurst. He wouldn't waste Anstruther's daughter on someone unimportant. But she could have met Hugo in other ways. If the German envoys believed the Secretary would return, they could set Hugo to charm the daughter.

He said, "You don't realize. You give your perturbation away. It haunts your eyes. And you've talked too long with me. Your friends are restless. What will you tell them?"

She smiled with her small mouth. It lighted her face for that moment, gave her the look she should have worn with her youth. "I'll tell them you are of the Secretary's office. That will excite them. They have a great admiration for my father." She added as she stood from the table, "They're both with Peace departments, English and German. I'll tell them all about you and they won't talk of my father."

He smiled down at her, asking, "Do you know anything about me?"

She nodded, solemn again. "I know more about you than you think, Mr. Hunt."

She was gone. He watched her go. And he watched the blond German rise, conquering, as she reached her chair.

III

There was nothing he could do for Bianca Anstruther. Not even warn her that her choice of companions, one in particular, was dangerous. He left the bar, went directly to the desk. The same carnationed clerk said, "Good evening, Mr. Pierce," and turned.

Piers said, "I have my key. Any messages?"

The man pried into the box. "None."

"My phone was ringing this morning, just after I left my room. I hadn't time to return."

The clerk said, "I'll ask the operator. She might have a record." He returned after a moment. "There was a call to your room but no name. I'm sorry, Mr. Pierce."

He said, "It couldn't have been important," and turned away to the newsstand. He saw the burly man then. He was standing against a pillar, his hands dragging in his pockets. He was incongruous in this sleek Broadway lobby. Piers turned back to the clerk. "I'd like to see the house detective."

The veneered mask cracked for a moment before it recovered obsequiousness. "Is there anything wrong, sir?"

51

"There is," Piers stated. "A man has followed me all afternoon. He is here now. I don't like it." He paused and his eye fixed the clerk. "I'd prefer that your house detective handle it. But if he doesn't, I will."

The clerk mouthed quickly, "Yes, sir. Certainly, sir." He didn't seem to know quite how to cope with this. He tinkled a bell and spoke hushed to the answering boy. "Will you find Mr. Sarachon at once?" His voice broke. "At once." He took his wine-colored handkerchief from his pocket and touched his forehead. "You should speak to the police, sir."

"I have," Piers replied. "Not two hours ago. Evidently the man was released with a warning. Evidently he knew where to find me."

Mr. Sarachon was dressed for the evening, impeccable, thinning hair, polished nails, soft black hat. A piece of Broadway, the aristocracy of Broadway. He didn't resemble his profession.

The clerk said, "Mr. Sarachon, this is Mr. Pierce. A guest of the hotel." He didn't know how to continue.

Piers took over. "There's a man who has been following me. Despite police intervention he has followed me here. I'd rather like it if you could get rid of him."

Mr. Sarachon asked as had the cop, "Why is he following you?"

"I don't know," Piers said wearily. "I've conducted government business all over Europe and Africa without ever having been followed." That wasn't quite true. "Now I'm on vacation, in my own country. I

52

don't know why he's following me. I don't like it."

Mr. Sarachon said smoothly, "I'll do what I can, Mr. Pierce. I can't exactly toss him out"—he showed his teeth and twitched his immaculate tie—"but in such cases a warning is usually sufficient. If you'll point him out."

Piers pointed. "The unpressed fellow over there."

Mr. Sarachon's eyelids drooped. He looked Piers over carefully before he walked towards the man, his steps brisk, assured. Piers leaned against the newsstand, took up a handful of evening papers, more cigarettes. He waited. He couldn't see Sarachon's face, only his mobile shoulders. The heavy jowls were shadowed by the crumpled hat. Piers waited. Sarachon's return was hesitant. He studied Piers obliquely.

"Well?" Piers demanded.

Sarachon rubbed the shine of his right hand fingers against his tuxedo coat sleeve. He said, "I'm afraid I can do nothing for you, Mr. Hunt. That man is Jake Cassidy. Detective first grade of the New York police force."

Piers took it slowly. He asked finally, "You knew who he was before you spoke to him, didn't you?"

"I knew he was Cassidy," the house detective admitted. "I thought he might be off the force, in private work, in which case I could have done something. However, he's still active, he showed me his card. I'm sorry. And the New York force—"

"I understand," Piers said. "Thanks just the same." He walked away to the elevators, leaving behind Sarachon's disturbed polish, the clerk's snide face,

Cassidy's imperturbable stance. Cassidy knew who the man was that he was following. The house detective had addressed him as Mr. Hunt only after he spoke with the heavy man.

Safe in his room he closed the door, leaving the room unlighted save by Broadway flares. He drew a chair to the window, sat there looking out and seeing nothing. He was being followed by a New York detective. Why? The question blinked with the lighted sign—why—why—why. Was it in connection with Johann Schmidt's death? Was it for some more important reason? If he knew for certain when Cassidy had picked up his trail, the answer would come clear. He had suspected a shadow after he left the precinct house. He had been certain of it after he parted with Gordon at the Chatham. If Cassidy had picked up the earlier trail, the visit to the police hadn't been as successful as he had thought.

Even so he could not regret the geste. Having his suspicion of Brecklein's delegation confirmed was worth whatever difficulties might now ensue. At least he could label the enemy. If, however, it had been Captain Devlin who in suspicion had set Cassidy on his trail, how had the detective learned the name was Piers Hunt, not George Henderson?

If his trail had been taken up later, with Gordon, it was easier to understand how he had been identified. Gordon had spoken over the office phone. Had the detective learned that and followed Gordon, he could pick up his quarry. This did not explain why the New York detective department should be interested in Piers Hunt. Unless Johann Schmidt had not died immediately, had existed long enough to exhale a man's name. There was no other possible connection between Cassidy and Brecklein.

If his own path were straight he could welcome Cassidy's supervision. God knows he needed protection. He couldn't afford its luxury as yet. He didn't dare come out in the open; he must continue to move secretly, to hide his real motives from all, even from his own associates. He could trust no one; no matter what dangers he was led into, he must walk alone. The end was more important than he.

The small face of the girl with lavender hair kept glimmering in the shade of his room. He had known that Anstruther had a daughter; he conceived of her as a little girl. It was a simple enough mistake. The Secretary had referred to her always as his little girl. He had mentioned schools: "I must be in New York before my daughter's vacation begins." "I must be home before my little girl returns from the country." Little girls grew up, a father didn't realize. Nor did a father's business associate. Piers hadn't realized that Bianca was a young woman. He regretted it; he wanted no women; the business was ticklish enough without this complication. His sympathy for her couldn't even be hinted. She would not forgive him for prolonging her anxiety, postponing her grief. It didn't matter save that she was Anstruther's daughter. After this was over he should like to help her.

He was tired. Another day gone but four yet to pass before he dared move. If he could be sure of success, the game would be worth its candle. He couldn't be. Not without Evanhurst or Fabian. There seemed little hope of Evanhurst. He moved from his chair, made a light and stretched himself on the bed. He went over the newspapers he had bought, rapidly, thoroughly. The delegation from Equatorial Africa wasn't mentioned. There was only one item worth attention, a noted Washington columnist, one whose comments were above question, had written: "Secretary Anstruther remains in retirement pending the opening of the International Peace Conclave on Sunday."

Piers pushed away the papers. If the commentator would look into Bianca's eyes his belief in his infallibility would be shattered. He flung away the newssheets; he might as well go out into the dinner and theater crowds. Dinner wasn't important but the theater would black out memory for a too brief number of hours. First a shower and change of clothes.

He pulled out the uppermost bureau drawer. He stood there, his hand tightening on the knob. The drawer had been searched. He opened each of the others in turn. They too had felt intrusive fingers. It was not that the contents were tumbled. It was rather the small disarrangement. Had not years of fending for himself in limited space given him an inordinate taste for order as against the time-wasting uselessness of disorder, he might not have noticed the intrusion.

He went without haste to the clothes closet. The suits as well. The spacing was different. He pulled out his two suitcases, large and small, opened each in turn. The linings were intact. He hadn't expected the consideration. Whoever had searched may have used a detector to make certain nothing was hidden. Yet a

finger touch could have told that no papers were se-
creted. Whoever had searched was after papers, the
papers of Secretary Anstruther. His lips curled away
from his teeth. They could have spared themselves
the deed. There were no papers here.

It amused rather than angered him that his room
had been searched. There was a bribe—if access had
been result of bribery—wasted. Entrance might have
been by a passkey, easy enough for one of the Smiths
to make one. He bathed, dressed leisurely. He put
on the dark suit again. It didn't matter its repetition,
not with his detective escort. Captain Devlin could
lay hands on him without trouble of search. He
pocketed his key, went out and walked the few steps
to the elevator. There was no life visible, no sound
here nor in the dim corridors stretching left and
right. It was as silent as if it were a dwelling place on
the Nubian desert. He touched the button again and
he backed to the wall where he might be safe from
surprise attack. The enemy had had access to this
floor at some time today. They could return.

The drop to the lobby was into a different world,
a world of cacophony and light. It was reassuring. It
even seemed safe. For a moment he hesitated, washed
by its disinterested safeness. He could remain here;
he didn't have to wander tonight. It was absurd to be
ridden by the hounds of fear on Broadway. Absurd
that he dreaded to emerge from his fox's hole, absurd
to fear the street because of an accident pattern that
must not be uncommon.

He had hungered for years to return to this garish
and, to him, precious sector of the universe. Crossing

he had believed that here he could forget the ordeal ahead, a week of losing himself on Broadway would give the necessary therapeutic advantage he needed before the hour of reckoning. He should have belonged to the theater world. His mother had been a Piers, yes, but she had been Cornelia Piers' own daughter. Not only had she married Horace Hunt, the leading character actor of his generation; she had not imported him into her world where he had no wish to be; she had joined his. Piers had been figuratively born in a trunk. That the trunk had been a luxurious one proved only that Horace Hunt had been a laborer worthy of his highly appraised hire.

Piers had been ten years old when he moved to Cornelia's. That was after his mother died. He didn't remember her well; he remembered rather Cornelia's portraits of her. Of what she had been there was for memory only the scent of red roses, laughter, the feel of silk. And the roses had been blighted long ago.

His father had died in the Last War. An airplane crash while he was touring the camps as entertainer. Piers and his father had remained good friends always; separated sometimes for years by Horace Hunt's moving-picture commitments, separated by a sequence of young and younger stepmothers, their friendship hadn't faltered. He had wanted to follow his father on the boards. He'd been studying, had even done summer stock and a Broadway walk-on before the war came. After the war it had been too late. It hadn't been important enough.

Only one thing had been important after that war, to work for peace. Luck had brought him to Samuel

Anstruther who needed young men with militant belief in peace to counteract the too many who passively accepted peace as their heritage. For twelve years he had been Secretary Anstruther's personal representative in Europe and Africa; Gordon had held the all-important Washington post. There were good men at the helm in the other districts but the under-leadership was divided between Gordon and himself. He was the man in the field, the trouble shooter called in before trouble could brew. There had been more trouble in the formative years, in those years before belief in peace, total peace, had been accepted. The past five years had been more or less uneventful. Man, even man in Government, wanted peace. Given assurance that he might have it, he had been eager to cooperate in its furtherance, far more determined than he had been in the past to cooperate in the cyclic necessity for war.

Until these border incidents had begun. The government of South Africa had reported them in March. It was undeniable that they had been fomented; the territory they spotted was too widespread for a mere local squabble. The instigators were held by Europeans to be of Equatorial Africa. That was the expected. What was not expected, what came in nature of a shock, was that Piers' independent investigating proved that only Germans had reported trouble. It was the sinister echo, out of the not too long ago past, of German voices howling of persecution.

He had waited for Fabian to speak, to report his finding to the commission. And Fabian had not spoken. That Piers could not understand. With charges made against his people, Fabian had blanketed Equatorial Africa in immutable silence. Piers' request for discussion with Fabian had been swallowed up in that silence. It was then, a fresh incident of purported butchery for stimulus, that Piers had secretly sent word to Secretary Anstruther asking him to confer with him in Africa. If any man could reach Fabian, it was Anstruther. If any man could see through the manipulations against peace, it was Anstruther. It was in the midst of this secret conference that the wire from Fabian had come. And Anstruther had gone to meet death.

With first report of the trouble had descended this enveloping depression. Piers knew history too well not to realize that war had more than once started from just such seemingly unimportant friction. Far more frightening was the presumptive evidence that the incidents were no more than smokescreen for the dread events shaping behind them, that there were deliberate plans for laying waste the world again in a holocaust of destruction.

It must be prevented no matter how many heads fell. He put away his dark thoughts. The heat of his mind must cool, give him respite in order to give him strength. He would go out, join Broadway. He started to the doors but seeing the ungainly bulk of Cassidy slouched against the same pillar, Piers diverted his steps.

He stood before the man. "Come along. We're going to do a spot of theater."

The little blue eyes sharpened. "What you talking about?"

Piers said, "I thought you might as well know. Dinner and the theater. You're coming, aren't you?"

Cassidy shifted his feet. "It's none of your business where I go, is it? Or is it?"

"You are following me," Piers smiled. "I'm just making it easy for you. I might get lost in the crowd, you know."

"Suits me." Cassidy studied his thumb.

"And me," Piers laughed.

"If you get lost," he put the side of his thumbnail between his teeth, "I'll find you again. New York isn't so big."

"I know," Piers admitted. "But there are hiding places."

"You'd come out by Sunday." Cassidy wasn't interested but he knew something he shouldn't know, that no one here should know.

Piers erased his sudden frown, spoke easily. "Can I stand you a drink before we start out—separately, if you prefer?"

Cassidy would have refused. He should have refused. Suspicion narrowed his eyes and he shifted again. But he'd had a long vigil and his feet must have hurt. There were no chairs here. The bar was near with sweet and acrid odors of stimulants and soporifics.

He said finally, reluctantly, "I could use a beer."

"That's better," Piers approved.

The man lagged behind him as if still following the letter of his orders. The bar was a little less crowded now, the dinner hour. There was no sign of Bianca Anstruther and her party. Cassidy pulled out a chair at a small table, sighed into it. "Bottle of Budweiser," he said.

"You won't mind if mine's an aperitif, Mr. Cassidy? I haven't dined." He directed the waiter.

"How do you know my name?" Cassidy wasn't at ease.

"I made inquiries." Piers laid his package of cigarettes across the table.

Cassidy struggled with deep thought. "That damn Sarachon. Used to play the drums in a band here."

"Perhaps." Piers held across a light. "I don't suppose you'd tell me why you're following me?"

"Who said I was following you?"

Piers' look was level and ironic. "I can't believe your private tastes are as catholic as the greensward of the park and the bar of the Astor."

Cassidy's knobbed hand cooled on the bottle of beer. He relaxed after he tasted.

Piers said, "I've followed men myself in my time. Perhaps that gives one a sixth sense." He sighed. "I presume now that I've spotted you there'll be a new man put on me."

"That don't make no difference," Cassidy said.

Piers sipped. "It surprises me that you should be the shadow."

"Why's that?" The demand was belligerent.

"I should say that the New York detective force would not be interested in my itinerary." He glanced at his watch. "Time for another beer before I push along." He beckoned the waiter, repeated the order. "As far back as mind serves, quite a way back that is —I was born in New York—I've never caused any trouble in this city. Not even a filched banana or a slug in a gum-vending machine. Yet I'm of interest." He softened his voice. "Or is it for my protection?"

"You need protection?" Cassidy watched the foam rise in his glass.

"My room was searched today. Is that part of the service?"

The detective grunted, "I don't know nothing about that." He didn't; surprise had quickened his face.

"I didn't think you did." Piers let his hand flat on the table. "It wouldn't surprise me if we were both being followed, Mr. Cassidy."

"Who'd be doing that?" the detective scowled.

Piers stabbed out lightly. "There might be others interested in Secretary Anstruther's whereabouts."

Cassidy pulled himself up in the chair. The mask was pushed from his face. Behind it was revealed a man of brain, a hunter of strength, stubbornness.

"I can tell you you're wasting your time." Piers matched the coldness. "I do not know where the Secretary"—he recalled caution—"is in retirement."

Cassidy belched. "I'm not looking for the Secretary." His little eyes peered from under his hat. "I'm looking for a briefcase." He began to laugh, choking with it.

Piers echoed, "A briefcase." Bewilderment must have shown on his face for Cassidy wheezed until a globule fell from each eye.

But there wasn't a briefcase. He'd invented it for Captain Devlin. And Devlin, accepting George Henderson, had set this watchdog on Piers Hunt. It didn't add up. In order to recover a briefcase Devlin wouldn't set a watch on the man who lost it. The answer must lie in Johann Schmidt. Piers repeated now, shaking his head, "A briefcase?" And he frowned. "Whose briefcase?"

The laughter was shut off like that. The little eyes were again chips of stone. "The briefcase of Secretary Anstruther."

Piers removed his fingers one by one from the stem of the wineglass.

"It's about so big." The gnarled hands moved. "Made out of alligator. Real alligator."

Piers had realized it with a rush of fury at his self-betrayal. The betrayal of the subconscious. He had described Anstruther's dispatch case to Devlin. He had been so certain that no one would believe he would retain that case, that he had done any more than return it to the Secretary. Because no one but he knew the Secretary was dead. If he'd ever owned a briefcase, if he'd handled any other—it was too late to retract description. More than ever now he wanted to learn who had set the detective on his trail. How to ask he didn't know. He parried, "Do you mean the Secretary has lost his case?"

Cassidy drained the glass.

"And do you mean to say," he gathered momentum, "that Secretary Anstruther told you in order to find it you should follow me?"

The mask covered the face again. "Who says I'm following you?"

Piers said flatly, "I don't believe it." He forced it upon the hulk of man. "I've worked with Secretary

Anstruther for years. If he'd lost something and thought I might know where it was, he'd ask me. He wouldn't ask the New York detective force to find it by trailing me. Who set you on me?"

"The boss."

"The Commissioner of Police?" He was the boss; Devlin had said it. And he was averse to murder. Johann Schmidt was a part of the answer. Piers hadn't killed the man. But he mustn't talk about it. First they must give him their knowledge. He paid the check. "I'm going to dinner now, the theater later. I don't imagine it will do any good to tell you I have no briefcase, neither of my own nor of Secretary Anstruther, and that you might as well go home and get a night's rest."

"Don't worry about me none." Cassidy wiped his mouth. "I'm obliged for the beer."

Piers left him standing in the lobby, worrying a tabloid. But the eyes above the paper were watching.

2.

On Broadway at night, glittering and noisy, he was not haunted by African desert, by silence and sun. He moved with the crowd as far as Lindy's, waited for a booth. No one here was concerned about the future of peace. They had peace. He ordered a steak dinner, watched the crowd thinning as curtain time neared. Dining alone was dining quickly. He would reach the musical before its late curtain. There would be standing room; that was important, to get inside the theater.

When he came out of the restaurant he saw Cassidy, a loiterer on the corner. Cassidy didn't appear to see him. But it proved Cassidy had spoken true; it didn't matter that his identity was disclosed. He would follow until he was led to what the boss, or someone behind the boss, wanted.

Piers knew this theater, knew the second floor exit to a catwalk leading to the producer's office. An office which would not be locked until after the final curtain and which would be unoccupied during that time. The producer clung to the wings whenever he had a leg show. The SRO sign was out. Piers bought a standing room ticket and turning from the window glanced back at the sidewalk. Cassidy was there.

The house lights were darkening as he entered. Cassidy hadn't followed as yet. There were the last moments of confusion of seating. Piers moved on up the red-carpeted stairs to the balcony lounge, went to the water fountain for excuse and waited there while the orchestra leaped into rhythmic frenzy. There were others who came up the steps but none lingered, none noticed him. All were in haste to be seated before the rising of the curtain. It was possible that Cassidy would not come into the theater, taking it for granted that Piers had gone to the hit show for the purpose of seeing it. It was even possible that Cassidy would take time to feed himself, the big man must be hungry by now. Not that Piers believed that Cassidy would in so doing leave the way clear for Piers to slip away unencumbered into the night. There would be someone watching the exits, a policeman on the beat, a cabbie who could use a slice of police favor, a theater doorman. Meantime, what of the watcher who was watching both Cassidy and Piers? If there were such a one, he hadn't as yet passed the detective to come after Piers. Perhaps he too was hungry and did not fear losing his quarry as long as Cassidy was in clear view.

Piers had choice of following his original plan, that of leaving the theater during the general confusion of intermission, or of disappearing now. Despite the risk of drawing the attention of an usher by immediate movement, it seemed advisable to move before Cassidy's weary shoes dogged after him. He wasn't actually worried about getting past the usher, he had glib excuses waiting on his tongue for his exit. It was the later questions that would be asked concerning him by Cassidy, by an unknown man in the dark.

He crumpled the cup and dropped it in the waste container. By the time of questioning he should be well away. The corners of his mouth tweaked. Cassidy had definitely stated he didn't care if Piers did escape him. Escape him he would. He walked then without haste, with definite purpose, to the left of the house. The usher stood at the head of the aisle, her eyes on the comedy team chanting on stage. Piers murmured as he passed, "Leo's office," and waited a moment for no response. His father had been one of Leo's first stars. He continued without haste to the door, opened it a slip and stood outside on the narrow passageway, high above the dark alley below. He moved quickly now, listening for the crank of the door opening behind him, but it was silent. He hadn't been followed yet.

He had a moment as he reached the producer's door but the knob turned under his hand. It was the same grubby little office, unchanged in twenty years. Even the shabby couch was no more shabby, with no more brown criss-crosses in the worn black leather. He took a breath before he opened the door into the small anteroom. It was empty.

Luck had been with him. There was now the immediate necessity of getting away from here. He opened this door a wedge, slid through. One dim bulb lighted the landing. He remembered three flights to the alley exit. In the death silence the iron steps reverberated to his careful descent. Only if he removed his shoes could he muffle the sound. That chance he couldn't take. It would stamp him with suspicion if anyone should enter on legitimate business. Moreover, it would hinder progress if he had to cut and run.

Cursing breathlessly he wound down the staircase until he stood in the almost complete darkness of the alley level. There was no sound from above. As he remembered it the alley was short, only a few strides to the street in back of the theater. Yet he hesitated before opening that door, fearing not Cassidy but another man who might stand outside. He didn't want to die. His hand was actually clammy when he touched the knob, drew the door ajar, guarding himself behind it.

He looked out into an empty lane. He moved without sound now; closing the door noiselessly, his walk was swift to the end of the alley. Before stepping from its narrow confines, he peered out. No one was waiting for him. It was a cheap street. Without theaters, a cavernous garage across, a small dingy restaurant, dark windows of theatrical shoes, tailor shops, leather goods. This end of the block was deserted.

Piers left the alley in one stride and moved towards Eighth Avenue. There was more danger in picking a less lighted thoroughfare, one as deserted as a village at this hour, and none too savory at best. Nevertheless, he had no intention of walking into Cassidy's grasping hands again. And if, as he believed, he had not been followed, he was as safe here as he would have been in Berne. He walked Eighth to 54th street. By that time he was certain he had escaped all trackers. For the remainder of the evening he was free to do as he should choose.

He had had no plan in mind when he planned escape, nothing more than the throwing off of the confines of surveillance. But now that he was out of the box he knew what he would attempt to do. He walked across town to Broadway again. He had no hesitation in hailing a cab here in the Fifties. The men who were watching him might bribe the cabbies in the vicinity of the Astor; they could scarcely cover the town. Not a town with as many cruisers as Manhattan.

"Grand Central," he said. "Lexington entrance."

He leaned back against the leather. He could relax for this interlude. He lighted a cigarette. If he had any lingering doubts of being free he would erase them in these final maneuvers. He paid off the driver and entered the station. He didn't go to the concourse; he followed arrows across the station and to the Biltmore exit. He went through the hotel, emerging on 43rd, and made his way to Park. The avenue lay wide and quiet save for the endless stream of traffic. He walked to the great white shaft of the International Building.

It was possible but not probable that there would be someone in the office at this hour. After ten. The imminent Conclave meant an inordinate amount of work. If there was someone there he could ask for information of little importance. He touched the night bell and waited.

The guard was a stocky man with suspicion gritted into his mouth. Piers stated, "I'm Thompson. Peace office." The night guard couldn't possibly know all employees of the Peace office even by name. "Mr. Gordon sent me over for some reports he needs." He edged the door as he spoke. He didn't want to remain longer on the street, not daring to look behind him, expecting the coincidence of Gordon himself passing on his way to some function or other.

The guard was less suspicious at mention of the office and at the magic name of Gordon the scowl smoothed.

"If you'll take me up," Piers suggested, "I have the key."

"You got to sign the register."

"Where is it?" Piers led away from the door.

"Over here." The ledger was on the elevator stool. Piers signed illegibly, Ed Thompson, and walked into the elevator.

"Plenty of work with that meeting coming up, I betcha," the guard volunteered.

"Plenty," Piers responded. "Anyone else here tonight?"

"No. But some of the girls didn't get away till after I come on."

Piers said, "Well, the International Conclave only meets once in two years. That's not too tough."

The man stopped at the 19th floor. Their voices sounded lost in the empty, cavernous building. "I hope they'll tell them Germans where to head in," the guard continued with violence. "Imagine them wanting the International Army moved out of their country."

"You're against it?"

"You just bet I'm against it. Do you know why they want it?" He scowled like a conspirator. "It's so they can start another war, that's why."

"I agree," Piers said.

"You bet that's what it is. All the excuses they can think up—my kid could see through them. Expense for the United Nations—what do they care? And that one about their pride being hurt! Ain't that too bad? After what they done in the Last War." He shook his head.

"You were in it?"

"Three years. I know what war's like. Maybe you don't know—"

"I had four years of it."

"You do know." The man's eyes met his. "I can't see these big shots arguing we ought to withdraw the army. I can't see it. Anybody with the brain of a little duck would know what's behind it."

Piers said, "I wish you were a delegate."

71

"I wish I was too. I'd tell them."

"Yes." His thoughts were long. If it were only possible for the men to be there, the men who had evolved from war. He shook out of it. "I'd better find those reports."

"Yeah. Gimme a ring when you want out." The elevator door slid silently shut, the whine of its descent diminuendoed.

He was alone on the 19th floor, alone in shadows flung by the night light. His steps on the marble corridor echoed as he approached the door. The key should admit him both to the office at large and to the private offices. It was Anstruther's key. It turned and he felt for the light before entering the austere anteroom. Light flooded. He knew then there was no one here; the room had the smell of emptiness. But it wouldn't be wise to tarry too long. It was entirely possible that there would be watchers to report an unexpected light in the Peace office at this hour. And there was always the coincidental approach of Gordon in his mind.

Gordon's door was lettered, not locked. He left it in darkness until he had closed the Venetian blinds, then turned on the desk lamp. The desk itself was locked; the files were open. He pulled the drawer E. Standing there, he read the Evanhurst correspondence, rapidly, photographically. There was no doubt that Evanhurst was committed to the policy of releasing Germany from supervision. There was little doubt that Gordon concurred.

He went quickly to B, Brecklein. There were the same arguments Anstruther had voiced, that the guard had stated. Withdraw—save expense to the United Nations. Withdraw—we have proved ourselves peaceful in these twelve years, why humiliate us longer? Withdraw—we can become self-supporting, valuable in trade channels if we are allowed freedom of production again.

Anstruther had hinted this. Why force Germany to ship out her metals when her factories could so easily manufacture at home? Under the international laws, of course, the laws of peace. Brecklein even dared mention the building of planes, quoting the superiority of the Luftwaffe in the Last War. The guard downstairs had said it. "Even my kid could see through it." But the kid wouldn't be blinded by personal ambition, by worship of the ape, by wish fathering the thought.

He should leave now; he'd found out enough to know where Gordon stood, enough to know it was wisdom to steer clear of Gordon's aid. But he went rapidly to the Schern file. Little here. The silent partner. He turned from the files. And then he forced himself to return to them, to open the file on von Eynar.

Surprisingly enough, what he had wanted was here. The border incidents. There was no doubt about Germany's part in them. For a moment he doubted the letters as genuine; this danger in an open file. But he realized, in themselves they were nothing. It was only by adding them to his own information that their treachery was fact.

He took the three most damning. It meant time, and the sweat stood cold on his flesh while he sat at the typewriter and copied the three. He traced a signature, Hugo von E. It would pass casual inspection. He put the copies into the file. He would never again hear the sound of a typewriter without remembering its unholy percussion in a deserted building at night.

The originals he put into his inner pocket. He turned off the lamp, opened the blinds, went through the anteroom extinguishing that light, stood again in the shadowy hall. No one could come in without the guard admitting him, but anyone could give a fictitious name and reason for entry. His empty steps jarred his stomach and he pushed the buzzer with a damp finger. His hair crawled while he waited for the whine to rise. Even when it ceased at the floor he was taut until he saw the same guard who had brought him up.

"All finished?"

"Thanks, yes." His forehead was damp. "Took me a little time but it's all right now."

"I had a bit of trouble myself," the man said. "Isn't often you get it. Not much excitement in this racket though my wife gets kind of nervous for me sometimes."

Piers controlled his voice. "What sort of trouble?"

"Fellow tried to push in, said he come to meet a Beers Hund here. Kept telling me this Hund was waiting for him."

Piers laughed a little. "Didn't get in on that one, did he?"

"You bet not." The car jolted to a stop; Piers didn't move from its safety. "I said there's nobody here. You

74

come around in office hours to see your man. And when he tried to talk back to me I just put my hand on his chest and pushed." He scowled. "Talked like a Hun. Beers Hund. If he comes around again I'll call the cops."

Piers was cautious. "Did he leave—after you pushed him?"

"Not right away. Guess he's gone by now."

He wasn't. Piers knew that. He was waiting somewhere outside, waiting for Piers to reappear. To follow again? Not tonight. If that was all he wanted he'd have been content to wait outside, not show his hand. This was more of the real thing.

Piers couldn't show his own hand to the guard. He'd come through too well up to now. Gordon must not know of this visit. There was no excuse to offer for prowling by night where he had access at any time. He had no moral way of obtaining a key. Yet he couldn't in sanity walk out into the arms of one of Brecklein's men. Perhaps the uncle of one Johann Schmidt. He had to play it quickly; he couldn't delay here with the presumptive reports for Gordon in his pocket. He bit his lip. "I wonder." He was confidential. "These reports are important to the Conclave. I wonder if that man could be a German who doesn't want me to carry them to Mr. Gordon."

The guard's black eyes clicked.

"He must have seen me come in. Maybe he listened in on Mr. Gordon's call to me. Germany doesn't intend to be turned down this time. She wishes to eliminate all chance of failure."

"Them dirty Huns." The guard's jaw squared.

"I must get out without that man knowing it. In case he's hanging around."

"We better call the cops."

"No." Piers spoke sharply. It could have been too sharply the way the man peered at him under the peak of his cap. "Don't you see?" Piers went on to explain. "That's the last thing I can do. That would mean publicity. It would give Germany something against our country, an incident, a hold over us. By the time we finished apologizing for having one of their men arrested, we'd be promising them withdrawal."

The guard growled, "Diplomats are too lily-livered. I'd like to see myself knuckling under to any damn Hun."

"We must preserve peace," Piers said. No matter what you'd like to do to those who threatened it.

"Then how you going to get out?" the guard asked.

"I don't know." He could call Cassidy to come for him. But Cassidy mustn't be allowed to report that he'd visited the Peace office. He asked, "Is there a phone?"

"Yeah."

"I'd better phone for a cab."

"You'd get one quicker standing outside." He shook his cap. "You can't do that though. If he's out there."

"I'll have to chance making it from the door to the cab. That's all I dare do."

The guard spoke with regret. "Wish I could get my

brother-in-law. He drives for Yellow. But he's cruising Broadway this time of night." He shook his head. "I know a checker at Yellow. I'll call his stand for you if you want."

"Thanks awfully." He didn't remain there in the empty hallway; he followed the guard to the switchboard. It was in sight of the glass doors. His neck crawled while he listened.

"Harry? This is Nick. I want a cab. Yeah, at the International Building. Tell the driver to keep the engine running and be ready to step on it. No— nothing wrong. For a friend of mine. Yeah, it's an emergency run . . . How's Thelma? . . . Yeah, she's fine. Yeah, that's right. Be seeing you." He disconnected the service, said to Piers, "Harry'll send you a good driver. I can't leave the building but I'll keep my eyes sharp till you get away."

Piers said, "I'm grateful to you, Mr. . . . I don't even know your name."

"Nick Pulaski."

They moved to the doors now, standing there silent, watching the muted flow of traffic. Flicker of lights up the avenue, their widening glow as they neared, the red circlets as they vanished. The sound of the tires was muffled here. There was no horn squawking, no squeal of brakes as on Broadway.

The guard said, "It'll take a little time. Harry's stand is over on Lexington. In the Sixties."

"It doesn't matter."

"Say, I never thought," the guard said. "We could have called Mr. Gordon."

"It didn't occur to me either," Piers said. He had folded a bill and held it out now. "Buy yourself a cigar and thanks again."

The guard shook his head. "I don't want pay to take care of a German."

"It isn't pay. It's for all your trouble." He urged it on the man. "Buy the kids a treat. There are kids?"

"Three boys." He took the bill. He looked at it, still reluctant. "I don't ever want them to see what I saw. I don't want them to know anything about things—things that happened. Bombs dropping on little kids—"

"I saw it too," Piers remembered. He added, "We mustn't let it happen again."

"We won't let it happen again." The man spoke violently. "No matter what the big shots do we aren't going to let it happen again."

But memories were short-lived, while greed and ambition flourished like the ancestral green bay tree. Piers said, "If anything should happen to me—"

The taxi was pulling to the door.

"I'll get the guy myself," the guard avowed. He unlocked the door.

Piers edged out. He ran for the cab. There was only the sidewalk to cross. It couldn't take more than seconds to reach the open cab door. But from the darkness against the building a squat figure also chugged towards the waiting taxi.

"Mine cab," the man grunted.

"Sorry." Piers pushed. His hand was on the door. He said to the driver, "Nick Pulaski called Harry."

The driver's ugly face said, "You're the one. I seen you come out of the building."

The squat man stood in the way. "Beers Hund—"

"Get out of my way. I'm in a hurry." Piers shoved the man off balance. He slammed the door as he stepped in, urged, "Go on, driver."

The squat man was standing there, impotent, his round face glittering after the moving wheels.

"Where to?" the driver asked.

"Just get out of sight. Then I'll give you directions."

"Trouble?"

"There could be." He felt in his pocket. The letters from Gordon's files were there. But of course, the enemy couldn't know he had them. It was something else they wanted. Piers was as winded as if he'd undergone physical, not nerve exertion. He wanted his room quickly, bed, but he didn't dare drive directly to the hotel. The squat man had doubtless memorized the license number. He rode in silence as far as 34th street. He spoke then, "I want to go to Grand Central."

"We already passed it," the eyes in the mirror reported.

"I know. I wanted to be certain we'd lose that man."

"Who is he?"

"I don't know." He'd never seen the moon face before. "I'm carrying some important papers. I'm with the Peace Department. How do you feel about peace?"

The brows scowled. "If they take the army out of Germany we'll have war again in ten years. You can't trust them Dutchies. They're as bad as the Japs. You don't see China letting Japan get any ideas of speaking out of turn, do you?"

Piers shook his head. "They are wise enough to be forceful for the preservation of peace."

If Germany could have been eliminated entirely as a political unit as Japan had been. But there was only one strong voice in Eastern Asia. China. In Europe there were too many.

They were approaching 42nd now. "Any door?" the driver asked.

Piers said, "I've changed my mind. I'll get off on Broadway. Lindy's." It would be as safe as taking the shuttle across town. The fat man might be watching Grand Central, expecting that maneuver. Broadway would be at its brightest, theaters opening their doors, taxis clustered, the police standing tall at every intersection.

He paid off the driver at the restaurant.

"Hope you don't have no more trouble," the man said. He purred away.

Piers didn't go inside the restaurant. He swung into the down stream towards the Astor. He was only mildly surprised to see Cassidy leaning against the newsstand.

Cassidy asked, "Where you been?"

"To the theater." Piers gathered the early morning papers.

"You give me the slip," the detective said without rancor.

80

Piers grinned at him.

"If there's been any murders tonight, you'll be hauled in."

"I'll produce an alibi," Piers assured him. He glanced at the bar. But he was too fatigued to risk an encounter with Bianca Anstruther tonight. Or with von Eynar. Or even Gordon. He said, "I'm going to bed. Don't you ever sleep?"

"It's nothing but a habit," Cassidy proclaimed. He was half asleep on his tired feet.

"I'm not going out again," Piers told him. "You'd better turn in. Good night." He went to the elevators, up to fifth, said "Good night" absently to the attendant. He walked the few paces to his door, set the key. He wondered what the squat man was doing now. He opened his room, closed the door after him.

"Do not make a light." The voice from the shadows was deep and it was cold. "What you see in my hand is a gun."

IV

The shadow was gigantic, dark against the room dark. The blinking sign across Broadway lighted again and Piers could see the man. He said softly, tentatively, "Fabian?"

"I am David. I am from Fabian." He wasn't giant. He was small and quiet and black as the night. "It is better we speak without lighting the room, Piers Hunt. Better we do not call attention to your room."

"Yes." Piers flung the papers on the bed freeing his hands. But he had no intention of moving against a man with a gun. "Won't you sit down?"

"No." The flickering light described him. The close-cropped graying head, the whiteness of teeth, the conservative English-tailored suit.

"May I? I'm tired."

"As you will. But where you are please."

Piers sat on the bed. He pushed back his hat. Weariness crept over him, bone weariness. This man came from the man he wished to seek as friend, came as enemy. "You might as well put down the gun," he said. "I'm not armed. I haven't been armed since the day of peace."

82

David said, "I could take no chance of not obtaining what I came for." He didn't put away the gun. It gleamed, now dull, now bright, in the whim of Broadway. It was like a toy in the black hand.

"How did you get into my room?" Piers asked.

"Through a ruse," David said.

"And you knew I was stopping here?"

"You have been followed."

"Yes." He began to laugh, weakly, silently. "God, yes." He forced a hold on himself. "Yours are better. I didn't know about yours." Africans from the bush. They would track a man and he would never know. He would die not knowing. "What do you want?" Piers asked suddenly.

"Secretary Anstruther's dispatch case."

"Why not go to him? Mind if I smoke?"

"I do not mind," David said. But the gun was steady until Piers had lighted and extinguished the match. The African said then, "Anstruther is dead."

Piers spoke with slow deliberation. "That information—if true—would be above value to many."

"Anstruther is dead." He was like a statue of carved ebony. Piers could see his eyes, dark and fathomless. "He died on the Nubian desert. He and the unknown."

Piers remembered then. Fabian was of Nubian stock. It accounted for a drum beating a message from ancient Nubia to modern Equatorial Africa.

"You know this?" Piers asked.

"I know this."

Piers spoke out in dull anger. "Fabian sent him to his death."

"Fabian?" There was measure of surprise, incredulous surprise, in the question.

"Fabian wired asking him to come at once to the Lake of the Crocodiles."

"Fabian sent no wire," the dark man stated.

"I saw it. Anstruther had planned to leave for the States. The wire came. He left instead for Equatorial with an unknown pilot, a German."

"This wire—what did it say?"

"It said that Fabian wished to see him. We knew it was the border incidents. Anstruther would do anything for Fabian. He left at once."

David said, "Fabian was in Tibet. He could send no wire from the Lake of the Crocodiles. Show me the wire."

"I haven't it." It was safe. "Fabian's name signed it."

"Fabian sent no wire," he repeated steadily.

Piers rose from the bed. The gun moved to cover him. "I want to talk with Fabian. I don't know why he sent it. He hadn't answered my request for an audience; he hadn't reported the incidents to the Commission."

"He did not need help; he preferred to handle the incidents himself. They were not important unless made so. Making them so would threaten peace." David paused. "Someone made use of his name. The plan was successful. Anstruther is dead. Why else was there a wire—if there was a wire—" His look was steady on Piers. "You have the dispatch case. You were seen with it in Alexandria. In it are the Secretary's final decisions for this conference. It was on these he worked in Alexandria. We wish to see them before the conference opens."

Piers breathed deeply. He knew now what he had actually known since last night. It was the Anstruther memoranda. His supposition, based on what he had believed at the time was rational, that anyone noting the case in his possession would take for granted he carried it to the Secretary, was not valid longer. Because Anstruther's disappearance had become established. "Secretary Anstruther carried his dispatch case on the flight. I may have been seen with my own, a similar one."

"Show me this similar one."

"I can't." He put his hands in his pockets. "I lost it. Last night."

The man's smile was ironic.

"I lost it on Broadway last night. There was an accident in front of the Paramount. A man named Johann Schmidt was struck by a taxicab. In the hub-bub my case disappeared. I reported it to the police today." He lifted his voice. "You can use that gun on me if you choose but I can't show you either Anstruther's dispatch case or my own. I have neither."

David put the gun into his pocket. "I did not come here to kill you, Mr. Hunt. I came to see certain papers. If you refuse to show them to me—"

"You can search my room," Piers said.

"It has been searched."

"Search me if you like." He remembered only then the letters he had taken.

"You could not carry that many papers on you. No." The head moved. "If you refuse now, we will wait. You will eventually lead us to where they are."

Piers' mouth thinned. He would lead and the bushmen, even in tailored clothes, would follow without so much as a faint footfall heard. He wouldn't lead Fabian to the papers. He had been forewarned.

He asked, "You're going?"

"Yes. There is nothing more I can do tonight." The telegram had muted the lion's roar. For tonight.

"Before you go——" He must know. "How will Fabian vote?"

David's voice was soft. "Only Fabian knows that. Only one man would he tell that. That man is dead."

Piers put out his hand. It couldn't halt this man but he put out his hand. He pleaded, "If Anstruther is dead, if you know this——" He didn't know how to say it. "Have you informed Gordon? The President?"

The eyes lidded. "We have told no one. We are wiser than that, Mr. Hunt. We will tell no one until Fabian has seen the Anstruther papers."

"Let me talk to Fabian. You can arrange it." His voice was on its knees.

"With the Anstruther papers?"

If he dared, but he didn't. Not until he knew where Fabian stood. Not with that wire engraved on his brain, not with a gun in David's hand. He said, "I don't have them. If I could talk with Fabian——"

"It is impossible."

Piers watched helpless as the man, soft-footed, jungle-footed, went away. He hadn't known, there distorted by shadows, how very small this man was, slight as a child if his hair was worn with gray. When he had gone Piers turned the night lock in the closed

86

door and he went to the window, threw it wide. He leaned out over the moving segment that was below. He watched for a long time.

The black man had come not in peace. He had come with a weapon of death in his hand. Yet Fabian was a man of peace. He must be that or the world tottered. The world was in peace. It remained in peace by force alone. Was there no way to insure peace among nations save at the point of a gun? A nation was men, many men, the minds and hands and spirits of many men. Couldn't man, all men, want peace enough that peace would be? An inevitability as once war had seemed an inevitability?

Slowly he drew himself back into the shadows of the room. It was too soon for despair. The world had made strides to the stars. Incredible as it seemed there had been no Secretary of Peace in any national cabinet until after the Last War. Always a Secretary of War, and a Secretary of the Army and the Navy, but no voice for peace until twelve years ago. Always the threat, always the expectancy of war. And the residue remained.

Through centuries of peace, peace must become as rooted as was war, only when that state was achieved could force be discarded. Was that Utopia? Was it too much to hope?

Too soon to get discouraged, too soon even if he were being hunted through the streets of New York, even if Anstruther lay dead in Africa, even if Fabian, his hope, had sent a man with a gun in his hand. Peace must not be threatened. He too could take up arms. He would fight for its preservation without

Fabian if that was how it must be. But his heart was sick within him. He knew how small he was, one infinitesimal man fighting alone. Courage and creed were not enough.

2.

The lights were a golden haze, reflected in the golden furniture, in the mirrors and their golden frames. A uniformed attendant took Gordon's tall silk hat, his white gloves, his ebony stick. Gordon didn't need to touch his white tie but he regarded its perfection and his handsome face, his glossy hair in the mirror. Piers was faded, someone who was reflected in the glass dimly, from afar.

Gordon said, "Don't worry about not dressing. I'll say you've only come over." His faint disdain touched Piers' grays.

Piers didn't care. Unreasonably he hadn't thought white tie or black when he dressed tonight. More tumultuous affairs had occupied his mind. Gordon would never have been that engrossed; it was part of his perfection and his attainment.

The manservant announced them softly at the door of the parlors. His voice couldn't have carried across the room but Evanhurst turned and loped forward. Piers knew the face, hammered leanly of aristocratic coin; he knew the tall form, aged to emaciation, the mustache, white now, which sheltered an unknown mouth. Piers stood behind Gordon, but it was he to whom Evanhurst extended his first hand.

"Piers. Piers Hunt. I'm delighted, my boy. What more can I say?" His left hand reached for Gordon.

"Witt, you're looking splendid, of course. Always splendid. And how good of you to find Piers." His voice rose and fell out of his high-bridged nose. He was an old man, Anstruther's generation. The crisscrosses of skin had been etched for many years in that same pattern. His eyes had faded, what once had been blue pigment was almost colorless. But he wasn't tired, as Anstruther had been tired. He was still a man who could fight with delicate fine-tooled weapons. He put a narrow hand under the arm of Piers on his right, of Gordon on his left. "It will make our evening more important. I've known Piers a long time, Witt, did he tell you? Since he was a small boy. In this very room."

Gordon thrust his head at Piers. Lord Evanhurst's high-pitched laughter enjoyed its moment.

Piers said in explanation, "This was my grandmother's apartment. I was brought up here."

Then the room had been somberly beautiful, dark oiled furniture, heavy raspberry brocades looped back from the windows. Now it was all white and gold. It was the Plaza's royal suite. It had been their royal suite then too, when Cornelia Piers reigned here. Gordon didn't know. He didn't know much about Piers and this information pleased him if it left envy. Piers' lack of dress wouldn't bother him now.

Lord Evanhurst shook his head. "She was a wonderful woman, Piers; I remember her in London when she was young. The toast of the King. That was George the Fifth—before your time."

He had led them across the room and the heavy man with the heavy porcine face rose from his white chair. He took the scented black cigar from his lips, thin lips in a heavy face. He thrust a manicured ham at Gordon. "Good-evening, Witt," he said. "How did you come out at the races today?" There was little accent; retention of foreign inflection alone.

"Rather nicely," Gordon responded. They were men of good humor, evenly met, not the American Undersecretary who might in a few days be the American Secretary of Peace, and the German envoy humbling himself for a favor.

"You know Ernst Brecklein, I believe?" Evanhurst asked.

"I don't," Piers said.

Evanhurst tapped Brecklein's arm. "Ernst, you don't know Piers Hunt?"

The big head turned slowly. He didn't put on the broad smile for a silent space. There was surprise in his narrowed eyes, surprise that almost hid the cold hostility beneath it. And then the smile cut through but the eyes weren't smiling, they were appraising this slight, unimportant-looking man in the gray suit. "I have not had the pleasure," he bowed.

"You know of each other certainly," Evanhurst pattered. "Mr. Brecklein, Mr. Hunt. Piers is an old, old friend of mine. I knew his grandmother well. Mr. Brecklein is acting as Germany's chief envoy to our present Conclave, Piers." He waved a fine hand to the small man who had slid beside Brecklein, who was now shaking hands with Gordon. A man who when he was young might have been brother to Johann Schmidt. He was dried out now, all but the wolf lift of his lips from his teeth. His hands had been

scrubbed white, how many scrubbings to wash away
the blood of the innocents which had eaten into the
flesh?

"Schern, you know Piers Hunt?" Evanhurst insisted. "No? An old friend of mine." Piers bowed, his
hands at his side. "I knew him when . . ."

The pointed tails, the richness of smoke and drink,
the gloss of the host couldn't take away the smell of
blood and burning. In his grandmother's parlors.

The girl on the terrace beyond, the girl with the
pale gold hair cupped over her shoulders and the pale
gold silk molding her young body was Bianca Anstruther. He couldn't see her face; it was lifted to
Hugo von Eynar. Piers knew then as he'd known last
night that he must meet Hugo face to face. He said
without disturbance, "There is someone I know,"
even as Gordon, tired of Piers and his grandmother,
cried, "There's Bibi. I didn't know she was coming."

Evanhurst cackled, "She dropped in. I believe she
has a message for you." He lowered his lip. "Hasn't
Anstruther come out of hiding yet?"

Piers followed Gordon's extrication to the terrace.
Gordon was holding Bibi's hand, reprimanding her.
"Why didn't you tell me you were coming here?"

Piers said, "Hello, Hugo."

Hugo von Eynar's yellow eyes were insolent. He inserted his eyeglass to cover one. Only Piers knew the
woman shape of that face. "Hello, Piers." The voice
was more insolent. "I scarcely expected to see you
here."

"I scarcely expected to be here."

The rope of hostility was stretched tight as it had

been in the past, as it always was to be. Womb enemies.

Gordon said, "You haven't met Bibi, Piers. Bianca Anstruther, Piers Hunt. Our Secretary's daughter, you know. And my fiancee."

"Yes. I used to wrap dolls to send her from Switzerland." The girl's eyes, blue purple eyes, violent eyes, were silent on his. He tried to smile. Gordon's fiancęe. Another knot tied in success.

"You met last night," Hugo stated.

"No. I picked up Mr. Hunt, Hugo." Bianca spoke clearly.

Hugo shrugged. Gordon frowned at her.

She continued, a faint smile on her small mouth and none in her eyes, "Of course I've known of him since I was a child. As he says, he used to wrap the dolls my father collected for me all over Europe."

Gordon remarked as if he couldn't forget it, "This once was Hunt's grandmother's apartment."

"It wasn't this splendid," Piers said. "It was old-fashioned." He broke off, turning to Hugo. "What brings you to New York at this time? I understood you were at the Embassy. Refugee from Washington's climate?"

"I am accredited to the Embassy." The yellow eyes were blank. "I am the ambassadorial representative to the Conclave."

Piers eyed him steadily. "The expert on the border incidents perhaps?"

Hugo's mouth was small and bland. "You seem to know. Perhaps you also know that our friends blame you for not keeping the peace in Africa. That too will be brought before the Conclave."

Piers shook himself out of thought. "There is peace in Africa, Hugo." He spoke lightly. "You surely don't think the border incidents are important, do you?"

Gordon turned his head as if he hadn't heard aright. "But they are important, Piers, rather disturbingly so. A threat—"

Piers laughed. "I've just come from there, old man. We don't consider them important. Fabian hasn't even appealed to the Peace Commission for investigation, they are that unimportant to him."

"But you told me, he wired Anstruther—"

Piers laughed again, at Gordon's protestant face, at Hugo's leashed anger, at Bianca's hostile young mouth. "I talked with one of Fabian's leaders last night. Fabian didn't send the wire; he was in Tibet at the time. Evidently some undersecretary—" The laughter froze on his face. "Or some interested party who wants trouble there."

Hugo put up the eyeglass against Piers' accusation. Gordon's doubt was worn openly. Piers stood, his hands in his pockets, relishing their enforced silence. Gordon could not ask questions, not and guard the secret of state. Von Eynar couldn't admit his prescience of the Fabian wire. Piers was certain it was German-instigated, even as he was certain that Germany was the coil behind the border agitation. Bianca was silent too, her hands clenched against the folds of her golden dress. Her eyes turned suddenly on Piers;

it was too sudden for him to hide the triumph which was flowing through him. He couldn't explain, not here and not yet. He could but accept the sting of her hatred.

Piers said, "Perhaps we should join the others? Private conferences aren't exactly cricket at this time."

He walked away as if the rooted enmity back of his back was without importance. And Hugo spoke behind him. "Perhaps you don't know that we visited Africa this year. Fabian was kind enough to invite us to his territory."

Piers didn't turn but the words had smote him as they were meant. That long ago the seed had been sown? Fabian in connivance with the Germans, with Brecklein's beefy assurance, Schern's guile? An understanding between Germany and the races of color? The idea was too evil to consider. For the colored races had the numbers, the resources. Under German organization and German wickedness, they could plunge the world again into a war whose ending must be the total annihilation of known civilization.

It was impossible that Fabian would be party to such a hideous debacle. Not Fabian, who was developing one of the great modern states out of primitive tribes, out of exploited peoples. Not Fabian, who had dreamed this native African state as important, as democratic, as modern as that of any white nation, who had in twelve years made giant strides towards its fulfillment. It couldn't be that he was consumed with ambition to the point that he would deal with Germany for continental conquest. It was anathema to that for which the name Fabian stood, not only in Africa but throughout the world.

Anstruther had believed in Fabian above all of the peace leaders. It was this belief coupled with his love for the African which had hastened him to the Lake of the Crocodiles following the wire from Fabian. To his death. His death of which only the Africans and Piers knew. And how many others?

Piers stepped into the lighted drawing room. The three followed from the terrace quickly now as if they feared to allow him to move alone. Distrust of him within hadn't vanished. None of the Germans had expected his presence tonight; none wanted it. None of the Germans wanted Piers here or anywhere. That was more of their superb espionage. They knew a man threatened even before he expressed his threat.

Evanhurst was greeting newcomers in the archway. Dessaye and Mancianargo. The dainty Frenchman, a shell, filled and emptied at Evanhurst's wish. Mancianargo, the bent Italian peasant, somber-faced, his gnarled wrists protruding from the sleeves of his old-fashioned dress coat.

Schern said, "Poor André! Shows his age badly." There was no pity on his tongue.

Brecklein's scorn gritted. "Who is the Italian?"

Piers answered him. "Humbert was too old to come. Mancianargo was Anstruther's choice. He believes in peace."

"Who doesn't?" Schern asked insolently. The smile of Satan was an arrow splitting his drawn face. "We in Germany above all hold to peace."

"I believed that Anstruther would be here to-night," Brecklein said. He said it to Piers and there was challenge in the twist of his smoldering cigar.

Gordon answered, "The Secretary was unable to make it. He seldom attends social functions."

Evanhurst, bright, birdlike in his age, was propelling the newcomers forward. He hadn't missed Brecklein's question. He said, "I hoped Bibi would join us in her father's stead. But she has more lively matters to attend, yes, dear?" His hand touched her hair.

"I must run along. Until later?" She divided the question between Gordon and Hugo but it was to the German her eyes turned adulation.

Piers' mouth tightened. He'd seen other eyes lift to the god. Hugo should not be allowed to corrupt Anstruther's young daughter. She moved to the door, lifted her hand in farewell.

Lord Evanhurst spoke with ancient courtesy. "Shall we repair to the dining room, gentlemen?"

The tapers, the heavy linen cloth, the bowl of white roses laid nostalgia on the table. Lack of honesty barred the spirit of Cornelia Piers. The secret currents seasoning the fine food, hatred and malice and wile, wouldn't have been permitted in her presence. This wasn't a table of peace. Not even when Evanhurst proposed the customary toast, "Peace be among you," was the devil's laughter silenced. There was no one here, save perhaps Mancianargo, who would fight for peace. And the Italian was without power, a minor pawn, representative of a nation almost destroyed in the Last War. Italy no less than France was dependent on Evanhurst.

96

"I too propose a toast," Brecklein said. "To Secretary Anstruther, who has done more than any other man for peace."

Piers' hand clenched the wine stem. He lifted the glass but he didn't taste. It was his laugh, and it wasn't a laugh, that broke the separate thought and knowledge seething in the silence. "It seems incredible that nations once planned for war as we plan for peace. Unbelievable that there once was a man named Hitler."

"He was mad, quite mad," Evanhurst nodded.

"Quite mad," Schern agreed thinly. "A strange genius. But then aren't all geniuses mad? Obsessed by the single idea."

Von Eynar said, "He put up a good show while it lasted."

"You knew him?" Gordon asked.

"Slightly, I'm afraid. I spoke with him only twice."

Piers stated, "Schern knew him well, Gordon. He headed the Berlin secret service, didn't you, Herr Schern?"

Schern's voice was colorless. "There were things necessary in wartime. As you know." He inclined his head towards Gordon. "You evidently are alone here in fortune to know nothing of such things. Lord Evanhurst sat in Churchill's council."

"I served with Darlan," Dessaye boasted.

"Piers, too, was in Berlin," Hugo smiled.

He stilled memory. "Yes. I hoped to come face to face with Hitler. Certain events canceled that."

Mancianargo hadn't understood much. His eyes had remained without light as the others spoke. Perhaps the name of the war-crazed leader of the Germans who had impelled the Last War, Hitler the Destroyer, awakened him. He said now, "There must be no war." Passion licked his tired face. "There must be no war again."

Evanhurst spoke to him gently in Italian. He repeated to the others in English. "It is the New World. We go forward with peace to security and prosperity." He lifted his glass.

Brecklein beamed and Schern relaxed. If Dessaye looked worried he would not speak. Gordon and Hugo nodded, well pleased. Piers alone sat sick in heart. Evanhurst was won to trust of Germany, to furthering her security and prosperity at the cost of threatening war again. His fists tightened under the table. Something must be done. The blind must be made to see. He was as silent as the Italian peasant while the others moved gambits of conversation through the dessert and liqueurs.

They returned to the gold and white room. He listened until he was stifled with the politeness, the commonplaces, the intrigue. Without apology he moved again to the terrace hung above the glade of Central Park. The black-green of trees flecked with golden bulbs of light, the pale luminosity of the tall buildings framing the border, the hum of the city rose to him. A wave of remembered beauty engulfed him. He had known true peace the first time he stood here. He heard the step and he swung about expecting von Eynar. Gordon stood there. Gordon asked, "Why did you refuse the toast to Anstruther?"

"You expected me to drink?"

Gordon walked to the parapet. He spoke out to the night. "Is he dead?"

Piers followed softly. He didn't answer until he pressed behind the man's shoulder. "I wouldn't say that aloud here. I wouldn't think it."

Gordon made a slow turn. "Is he?"

Hard anger thrust Piers. "That's what *they* want to know. That's what they're wondering behind the smokescreen of their fat cigars and their platitudes of prosperity and peace." He took a breath. "If they could know . . ."

"You're referring to Brecklein's commission?"

"To the Germans, yes."

"You're mistaken, Piers." Gordon was reasonable. "Germany wants only the freedom of the just."

He laughed the laughter of desiccation. He said, "You've listened to the siren song. Who sang it, the industrialist Brecklein, or the aristocrat Hugo? It doesn't matter who. The composer was Schern. I've known Schern a long time, Gordon."

"You're wrong, Piers. You're obsessed with the single idea. Your insinuation to Hugo on the African business showed that. You persist in seeing Germany as she was before the Last War. You don't recognize the aspirations of the new Germany." Echo words instigated by those within.

"I take it you are for withdrawal then."

"Definitely. I am for a great expanding world."

"And our Secretary?"

The doubt came into Gordon's eyes. "I don't know

for certain. He went to Europe to see for himself before deciding. Breck believes he favored them, he was well pleased with what he saw."

He would be shown only the greenest branches, not what roiled below.

Piers stated flatly, coldly, drawing the sword without fear between himself and the man, "I am for the letter of the protectorate. I believe that Germany must remain a dependency for the prescribed fifty years." He didn't fear while he spoke the words, because he was right and Gordon was wrong. He couldn't hope to convince Gordon in these few days against the long-studied blandishments of the Germans. He could only have faith that his truth would be conviction. But before the words faded, a chill of apprehension was laid on his back. He turned and he saw Hugo motionless in the doorway. Gordon called, "Come on out. We're catching a breath of air."

Hugo moved forward, his hatred of Piers covered by his grace. Because Gordon's conversion must not be threatened, because Gordon must not know what lay behind the masque and beneath the buskin. Hugo's lips smiled. "Gordon, we're awaited in the Persian Room. Bibi rang up. The old men are deep in figures and you know how figures bore me." He fingered his monocle. "The Arabic variety, that is."

Gordon laughed, any faint doubt that might have been implanted was scattered in the sun of Hugo. He suggested, "Join us, Piers." Not wanting it; it was a required courtesy.

Hugo did not add invitation. His hostility glittered near the surface in that moment. Possibly he sensed Piers a rival again, for the young Bianca this time. If Hugo could actually in this hour be interested in a woman— He could not; only for purposes of state.

Piers refused. He'd had a bellyful for this night. He followed the others into the drawing room; Brecklein and Evanhurst were talking, the other men listening.

Hugo said, "Will you forgive us, Evanhurst, if we join the ladies below for a bit of music?"

Evanhurst was quick on his cranelike legs. "Certainly, certainly, my boy. Not much amusement here for young blood." He splattered his old-fashioned politeness on each of them separately and in group. Piers might as well take his departure while it was offered. It would not be wisdom to remain here. He couldn't for long without speaking out and it wasn't time yet for that. There would be no chance for him to inherit Anstruther's place in the session if this aggregate of representatives was massed against him.

Evanhurst patted his shoulder. "I want to see you soon, Piers. To repeat old tales and memories, heh? How about lunch tomorrow? No, that's tied up—"

"Make it breakfast," Piers suggested. He too wanted to stir memories. Not of childhood. He watched Hugo and Gordon arm in arm pass through the arch. "I'm stopping here. You can ring me when you're about."

"Breakfast. Capital. Nine-thirty. No need to call. If you'll be up by then. You young lads—"

"Not so young," Piers said. "I'm turning in now."

He wondered about the detective who must have followed him this day. Not Cassidy. Cassidy was on his twenty-four-hour leave. Piers didn't know which face it was; there'd been little work for the man. He'd remained in his room until time to join Gordon at the Waldorf. Would the new man be in the corridor outside or, banking on Evanhurst's high respectability, be waiting below? He'd have a long wait. Piers didn't need to return to the lobby. He had the key for his room with him. In the room were the necessary items Abercrombie had delivered.

"Breakfast then," he said. "Here?"

"You wouldn't like to stay on a bit if you aren't dancing? Brecklein's giving us some figures on Germany's progress. Gad, what they've accomplished! Fascinating. Even under the protectorate."

Evanhurst was committed. The international protectorate was a barrier to a world he once had known, expanding trade. Hope of opening his eyes was dim. But there was still the hope. "Rather not," Piers said. "I'm not official. Watkins in town?"

"Washington." Evanhurst tittered. "Handling the heavy work." He didn't care much for Watkins, a plodder, without rank. "Breakfast then."

Piers said, "Good night, sir." To the others he spoke a general farewell. A frieze of faces, expressionless, dangling in time, waiting his departure to come to life again in their separate evil and innocence. None wise, not wise enough to realize that it was not Piers who was in danger; it was they and for what they stood.

3.

The corridor outside was empty. Below a man with an unknown face would continue to wait. It didn't matter, the man had nothing else to do. In the dark jungle outside other men with unknown faces skulked. Nor did they matter. This night he was not prowling into the arrows of danger.

He hadn't lost his nerve. It had been unshaken by Johann Schmidt; it remained steady after the encounter with the fat-faced Uncle Schmidt last night. Facing Schern with the corpselike hands, watching Brecklein's cruel mouth tighten at him didn't disturb him. He knew too well how much they had at stake. He knew as well that he alone had both the means and the will to thwart their plans. And because they sensed this, they had marked him to die. They would have no ethical hesitation about murdering him. The end, no matter how blood-crusted, justified the means in furthering German interests.

Basically it was that belief which had started the Last War. It would be a variation of the same which, were they successful, would precipitate the world into the throes of death. A next war would be a war of extinction. The refined details of mass destruction had improved in twelve years, and in the Last War extermination had been plausible if not effected. Germany must be held supine until her warrior breed had been eradicated by age. He could see no other promise for a world of peace.

The corridor below was empty of shadows. He turned the key and opened the door. The room was strange; it was as if he had wandered into Cornelia's servant wing by error. With the light on, he examined the clothes closet, the bathrobe, bed slippers. In the bureau drawers were the pajamas and other essentials. He must remember to leave a bill for the valet. He opened the window wide. There was no bright spectacle of Broadway outside, only the dark distances of the park. He turned from it. It was too dear; it betrayed the years of his insistence on forgetting all things quiet and kind and at peace.

He flung himself down on the bed. Not by peace was peace to be attained as yet. A man must still draw his sword before peace could follow. They were determined. They were so damn clever. The way they'd instigated these border squabbles. An incident could be integral, but a series of incidents spotted laterally across the border of South and Equatorial Africa was not. And their dirty hands were covered. But with those letters, he had the proof. It must be presented to the Conclave; he must have a voice in the Conclave to proffer them.

Fabian could know the truth. If David had but come as friend, Piers could have given him the letters last night. But he dared not mention them. David would have taken the letters by force had he known; they could disappear to suit the aims of the powers. Even as Anstruther's final memoranda would disappear if it could be found.

The fear was in him anew that the Germans had reached Fabian; only they could have set him after the dispatch case. Clever, cold, ruthless, above all clever. Three men. One the smart business man, one the sly diplomat, one the social ornament. A man for each man at the conference. For all but one man, the man of peace. And Anstruther was dead.

Fight cleverness with more cleverness. Yes. But Piers wasn't clever; he wasn't versed in wile. Fight cleverness with violence. Yes. Fight with the men of peace, the incorruptible faces and words exorcising the lemans of bestiality. Where were those men? A night watchman, a taxi driver, Piers. He was without power. This was Gordon's territory. Anstruther could not speak again for him.

Anstruther's living voice was never to be stilled. Piers would see that Anstruther spoke from the grave.

The telephone jarred him. He reached to the bed table, lifted it and held it for a long moment to his ear before he spoke.

Gordon's warm voice came over the wire. "Why don't you come down, Piers? Join us. Everyone's asking for you."

"I'm certain Bianca is," he said dryly.

Gordon was soothing. "She's just a child, Piers. And she's wrought up. No word, you know. He always kept in touch with her, a cable every Sunday when he was away. When it didn't come last week, she began brooding."

"She blames me."

"Because you saw him off, the last man to see him. I shouldn't have told her that, I suppose," he apologized quickly. "I thought it might help her if she could talk with you. You could tell her he wasn't in any danger."

Piers interrupted. "Do you have his papers?"

"What's that?"

"His papers. His dispatch case of papers."

"Do I? Good God, Piers, are you drunk? How could— He always carried it with him."

"I just wondered," Piers said. "There are a good many who seem to think I have it." He broke off. "I don't want to talk this over the phone. I won't join your party but when you can make an excuse, come up."

There was hesitation. Bianca was Gordon's fiancee but she worshiped Hugo. Gordon couldn't clear out. And he, Piers, was a witless one to believe that further discussion with Gordon might be of value. Gordon was saying—Piers could see the handsome frown, the indecision in his bitten lip—"I'll go back to the table and see what I can do. If it's possible, I'll be up."

Piers spoke the number. "Turn right." He replaced the phone. He ran his hand through his hair, down his narrow cheek. There could be no harm in letting Gordon know some of what had happened since his arrival. He might yet have to call on the Peace offices for protection. Even if that were not necessary, words spoken might well be carried where they would increase in power. The enemy could know that he was not blind to their attentions. Exposure could not dissipate these; it could force a change of means and in so doing deflect the aim.

He hung his jacket over the back of a chair, pulled off his tie and shirt and flung them there. He wouldn't take any chance on Gordon persuading him to come downstairs. He told himself it was that he didn't want to face Bianca's hostility again tonight but he knew the truth. He couldn't stomach Hugo's smile, and the knowledge of the past in that smile.

The knock sounded on the door and he swung it open. He stood there, his hand tightening on the knob, not moving. The expectation had drained from his face, leaving it parched under the protective brown coloring.

He said bitterly, "I've been expecting you."

She was fair as remembered. The veins in him ran warm as wine even as his hatred of this warmth clenched his guts. Her good height, her fine long bones, her heart face and the smooth cap of ochre hair, her eyes blue as a child's, wise as those of a witch. She looked as if the wind blew through her, clear and honest and sharp. Honesty had no place in her. She had been learned in the use of every inch of her loveliness when first he knew her. The years had enriched her wisdom. And yet she was changeless.

She said, "And I thought I would surprise you, Piers." Her voice was crystal. It was as deliberate a part of her as the golden lashes she lifted, as the way the room quivered when she crossed to the windows, graced the hotel chair.

He was wooden watching her, remembering her and hating the betrayal of his memory. She kept her eyes on him until he jerked the door shut with a vehemence that would have closed her out instead of in.

She said, "You wouldn't come to me." Her hands moved. "I have come to you."

He said again, "I expected you. When I saw Hugo,

when I knew Schern was here." His mouth twisted. "You're still his . . ."

"I am Frau General Brecklein."

He murmured, "Congratulations," and he said, "You forget that military titles are no longer in vogue, Morgen." His frown narrowed. "Or has Germany adopted them in advance of a Conclave decision?"

There was anger, a flush in her throat. "I do not know what you are talking about."

"Don't you?" He wouldn't sit down. He dared not rest on the edge of the bed lest remembrance overpower his senses. He walked back and forward, as far from her as possible, near the door, the escape. "Don't you?" His voice raised in spite of himself. "Which one sent you to me?"

"Sent me?" There was a quiescence about her, her hands motionless on the fragile white lace of her skirt. "No one sent me, Piers. I came because I wanted to see you."

His voice struck at her. "And why did you want to see me?"

"Because I loved you once," she said simply.

His knuckles were white. "You don't know what it means to love."

"I loved you once," she repeated.

"You think love is something to sell. To the highest bidder. And the bid was high, wasn't it? Congratulations, Frau *General* Brecklein." He had propelled himself blindly to her, almost without knowing it and certainly without willing it. His fingers burned into her shoulders. She didn't move. "God knows it must have been high when Brecklein could win over

Schern." His fingers tightened as he pulled her out of the chair against him, his mouth on hers. His revulsion flung her from him. She swayed slightly. There was a spot of blood on her under lip.

His voice came thickly. "You have what you came for. Now get out."

She put her smallest finger to her mouth, touched it, and looked at the dull smear. Her words were muted. "I haven't what I came for."

He was without emotion now. "I suppose it's the dispatch case."

She sat down again. "Why do you battle against the inevitable, Piers? As always."

He said, "Because I do not intend to foster the inevitability of a next war."

"You think that Germany would foster war? How can you be so dense? After what has happened to her in the past, she of all the nations fears any incident, no matter how slight, that could bring again such conditions."

He looked at her dispassionately. "You think I might believe those words because they come from your mouth."

Her hands moved on the white lace. "Hasn't Germany endured enough? Hasn't she been ground into the dust? Terms—"

"Don't bring up the Versailles Treaty." It wasn't laughter in his throat, it was something raw, ugly. "If there'd been realists instead of Fauntleroys at that peace table, we'd never have had to endure the Last War. This time we've done better, if it isn't undone."

"You are unfair." She turned her round blue eyes

up to him and he stiffened. "Your hatred of Germany is because you identify the country with me."

"That isn't true." He spoke as softly as she now and as directly. "What was between you and me was between you and me. I have never confused its privacy with the affairs of nations, believe me, Morgen. I haven't that mania of the ego. What is behind what you call my hatred of Germany is between Germany and my generation. And believe me it isn't a hatred of what a simple German must see when he thinks Germany. Not of her little homes, her streets and her villages, the beauty of the banks of the Rhine and the different beauty of Berlin. It is, I believe—I haven't analyzed it before—a hatred of her men to whom those things mean nothing, a hatred of those who have not blood but greed in their veins, who have ambition rather than spirit. A hatred of those who see Germany only as a sword to conquer, to crush smaller nations and greater, to whom Germany is a latent octopus whose tentacles, if fed, could encompass all of Europe. I have a hatred of German warriors, Morgen, those who mourn Hitler's death because they haven't yet discovered another pawn to take his place. And when they discover another—"

"That's a fine speech."

"It wasn't prepared." He lit a cigarette. His hands were shaking.

"You admit your hatred of Germany."

He said, "I'm afraid you didn't listen attentively. I hate the Hitlerian remnants who still believe he was a great man, a genius who failed only because he was mentally unbalanced."

"There are no Hitlerian remnants, Piers." Her look was honest but he knew the lies her honesty could cover. "There is no one who is fool enough to believe that."

His eyes slanted in mirth. "You should have heard Herr *General* Brecklein and Herr *General* Schern— and your beloved Hugo a few hours ago."

"You're lying." There was a grave anger on her mouth.

"I only wish I were," he said.

She held out her hand. "I would like a cigarette."

He extended the package at arm's length. With the light he came no nearer to her than was necessary. It was too near. He remembered the scent of crushed roses, the petal touch of her flesh. He saw again the curve of her throat, the dark ivory between her breasts. He shook the match from his scorched fingers and he turned his back on her, returning to stand at the door.

The smoke curled from her lips. "There is little doubt that you refuse to allow Germany to hold up her head among nations again. You will oppose the freeing of Germany from bondage."

"What bondage?" he demanded. "What has she to complain of? She can eat, sleep, build, create—in short she can do everything save manufacture instruments of war. Is that bondage? If she had been treated like Japan—or would you free Japan from bondage as well?"

She shrugged. "That is different. An island of aborigines."

"The Japanese might argue differently. But we

need not worry about their protesting. The Asiatics are wiser than we. They have made certain Japan will not foment another war. What has Germany to complain of? She's better off physically and economically and spiritually, yes, than she's ever been. Why is she so determined to rid herself of the International Protectorate if she has no ulterior motives?"

"The humiliation."

He laughed once, short, scornful. "A nation must know humility to be humiliated. I'm afraid that argument doesn't talk."

She watched the pale blue of smoke. "There is nothing could change your opinion?"

He was silent a moment. His mouth was cruel when he spoke. "Why not? Perhaps your husband's permission to return to my bed."

She rose and her mouth was rimmed with whiteness. "I should have known what you would be. You alone never sought me when you were in Berlin after the war. You couldn't forget the fortunes of war."

A knock sounded behind him. He ignored it. He said, "I thought love was stronger than war." The knock was more peremptory. He twisted a smile. "But then, I thought it was love." He swung open the door silencing her pale fury.

Gordon said, "I wondered what was keeping you, Morn."

One look at him and Piers knew how they'd got Gordon. The man might have planned to marry the Anstruther girl. He might once have had devotion for Bianca. But he was lost, hopelessly lost in Morgen von Eynar. He was, there in the doorway, ravaged by jealousy of Piers' presence in the room. The moment passed as he touched his cuffs, his tie. He saw the imperfection of Piers, his shapeless hair, his undershirt. He saw Morgen's perfection.

"I was just coming down, Witt." Her mouth was tender, and her eyes. "Piers refuses utterly to join us."

Gordon, reassured by her mask, turned to Piers. "I didn't know until tonight that you knew Morn in the past, Piers."

"No?"

Gordon was lost, lost in her expertness, in her changeling delights of love. As Bianca was lost in Hugo. Two innocents, for they were that despite their modern sophistication, no more than innocents in the hands of the von Eynars. He could no more warn Gordon than he could Bianca. Both would have to suffer experience. Perhaps it would give both more tolerance if not more wisdom.

"She wouldn't let me mention her name on the phone. She wanted to surprise you; she's just in from Washington. You were surprised?" He turned to her. "We're going over to Sherman's for a nightcap. You're certain you won't join us, Piers?" He didn't want Piers to accept. He wanted nothing but Morgen. It explained his haste to leave a conference of important men tonight, his reluctance to come upstairs to confer with Piers. It hadn't been Bianca. It explained his proselytizing for the side of Germany. Echo mourned: Lost, lost.

"No. But I thought you were coming up to talk over the briefcase business with me."

Morgen laid one lovely thigh over the arm of the

chair. "I didn't know there was business, Witt. I shouldn't have delayed you by talking old times."

"It can wait," Gordon began.

"But no." She was gentle and immovable. "Hugo taught me early never to come between a man and his business. He would not forgive me if I forgot a lesson. I will be quiet with my cigarette."

Gordon frowned at Piers. "It can wait till morning, can't it?"

"It won't take a minute now," Piers said and he wondered with self-scorn if his insistence was to keep her here longer in his sight. He couldn't talk to Gordon in her presence as he could alone. More probably his reason for delaying their departure was to watch Gordon squirm, to watch another man eaten by desire of one woman among all.

He thrust his hands into his pockets. "There seem to be certain elements in this city who believe that Anstruther entrusted his dispatch case to me." He relished the apprehension swift on her face. She believed he was going to give her away to Gordon. "Why, I don't know. The Secretary never lets it out of his hands. You know that. Perhaps, however, their reasoning runs that Piers Hunt wouldn't be here without a purpose. The most likely purpose would be to carry some messages for Secretary Anstruther. Going beyond that to the fact that it would profit a good many of the powers to know in advance what the Secretary will have to say in the Conclave."

Gordon had been afraid too, afraid he would give away too much.

"And that therefore, with additional precaution,

the case was entrusted to me who wouldn't be suspected of carrying it. Mind you I'm not saying this is the reason. It's merely my fancy on the matter."

"You asked if I had it?" Gordon queried.

"If Anstruther entrusted it to someone it must be either you or I, Gordon. It isn't I. It must be you."

"I don't have it."

"I'm sorry." He looked straight at Morgen. "It would have helped if you had. I could have said, Go chase De Witt Gordon. He's your quarry."

The anger raged again in her but she said nothing.

Gordon said, "What makes you think there are people after the Secretary's briefcase?"

"I've been followed."

He frowned. "That sounds melodramatic, Piers."

"Piers is melodramatic," Morgen said lightly.

He shrugged. "There's a nice problem there. Is a man melodramatic because of accident of birth as he is sanguine or phlegmatic, blue-eyed or square-jawed? Or is a man melodramatic because he is too often confronted with the situations of melodrama?"

She interrupted, catching Witt's hand. Impatience bubbled to her lips. "Let's go. Piers' father was an actor, you know. Sometimes that accident of birth is uppermost in him."

Gordon was caught between their rapiers. He didn't know but he understood a little. The shell of social intercourse had been cracked. He said, "I want to go into this more thoroughly, Piers. Can you give me a ring at the office tomorrow when you're free? Any time. I'll shift appointments. You know that you've been followed?"

115

"Definitely."

"And that your followers are after Anstruther's dispatch case?" His credulity was strained.

"That too." Piers grinned at Morgen. "I asked."

Gordon shook his head. There was something wrong, terribly wrong, but he couldn't discuss it now, not before Brecklein's wife. He wasn't that completely lost—or he didn't want Piers to realize it. He murmured, "Of course Anstruther wouldn't let the case out of his hands. I don't know why it should be thought that you——"

She said it then, what she'd wanted to say since she had come but which Piers had deferred by keeping her at bay. "Because it was seen in Piers' hands after Anstruther left the airport."

Gordon turned his amazement first on her, that she too should know of the case, then upon Piers and suspicion went with it.

Piers spaced his hands. "You mean one of such proportions, in alligator?" Both were measuring him. "That was mine. Very like Anstruther's. A hired observer might have made the mistake." He smiled a little. "In fact, two hired observers seem to have made the mistake."

"Where is that one now?" she demanded.

Piers spoke gently to Gordon. "My room has been searched. I didn't mention that. Expertly." He flicked Morgen with his eyes. "I left it in Berne, with Nickerson. And its contents. I'm on vacation."

She didn't believe a word of his lies but she couldn't make an open issue, not with Gordon here.

Gordon, the fool, said, "I never knew you to carry a briefcase, Piers."

He answered easily, "It's an acquisition since your last trip to the continent." He dismissed them then. "I'll ring in the morning. If you can squeeze me in—"

"I'll arrange it." Gordon's face was somber. He had touched Morgen's arm but he did not feel the flesh and bone, his mind was divided at this moment into too many other compartments. He wasn't lost completely then, his disinterest in women as interference in his career was still present. It wasn't the way a man should touch this woman. She would change it when she was alone with him, at the moment, strangely enough, she too didn't know. It wasn't like Morgen von Eynar to be unconscious of the attitude of one of her victims. She didn't know because it was Piers she watched, her mouth parted, but she withheld the words. She remembered at last who she was, what she must be. She laid her fingers on Gordon's wrist, her voice was right, careless enough, eager enough. "Can't we meet soon, Piers? There's so much to say."

He opened the door wide. He said, "I'm afraid I have no time, Morgen. And nothing more to say."

He shut them out. Let her explain that to Gordon. Let her explain away his rudeness and the look on her fine face in the teeth of it. She would. And Gordon would accept her explanation. Before they reached the Persian Room she'd have him convinced that Piers was in possession of Anstruther's case. He didn't care. He wasn't. He'd destroyed it. And the photostatic copies of the Anstruther papers were safe until he was ready to make use of them.

He undressed and he lay in the darkness without sleep, without hope of sleep. The sickness for her ate into him. Any fool would believe that twelve years was a long enough time for forgetting. Twelve years had been as nothing. She stood before him, he saw her, heard her speak; he smelled and touched her, tasted her.

And the sickness for her ate into him like decay. Why had she come? Not for this, not to unman him. Not even Hugo could believe after what had happened that Piers could again be witched by her. No one should know that the years between were nothing, that he could now—were it not for the hatred in him—grovel to her. She would not know that. That she had stirred his senses, that she would realize, for that was her trick in trade. But with the knowledge would be awareness of the revulsion she had aroused in him. She would never know that he lay here in the dark, parched with the wanting of her. There were other women. Women of beauty and pride and tenderness. For him there was Morgen.

Why had she come now? He walked to the window and he sat there in the chair that had held her. He needed all his strength for what lay ahead. He needed his full mind, uncluttered thought, wit and iron nerve, and nervelessness. He didn't need a woman. He didn't need the memory of a woman who burned the soul out of a man and shucked away his carcass. He didn't need the memory of a woman who lied with her mouth and the turn of her wrist and the movement of her bones. She could never do to him what once she had done. He knew her treachery and her barrenness. Knowing, why must he suck at memory to assuage his terrible want of her? Why had she come? Why had she come? Why hadn't she died twelve years ago in those last merciless bombings of Berlin?

He had loved her. After her he could not know love of woman again. He was lost because his love was for evil; he could not be satisfied with good. But he was too sane to return to evil, too proud for self-destruction. He would avoid seeing her again. It shouldn't be difficult. The Germans didn't want him in on the preliminary conferences. They might, with Gordon's words corroborating his, give up the idea that he was in possession of the briefcase. They would certainly, after she carried back his message, be more careful in their surveillance with the surveillance known to him. They were too wily to take any chances at this time on alienating even an unimportant member of the Peace Department of the United States of America.

He wouldn't think of her again. He'd eliminated her from conscious memory for twelve years; he could do it again. He sat there at the window until the city was silent beyond in the dark. Until the hunger in him for Morgen von Eynar was exhausted, and exhaustion emptied him of all but choice.

V

An ape grooming his tail. Evanhurst in a dressing-gown striped of purple and red and golden satin playing with his morning cup of tea, his reed-like Virginia cigarette a finger between his lips. It wouldn't be difficult to get rid of Evanhurst, a pellet in his tea, a doctored cigarette. Schern wouldn't hesitate if he wanted Watkins to take over.

Piers folded his napkin in his hand. He said, "I was there. I know the border incidents are incidents, no more. There is no need to send the International Force in."

Evanhurst mulled, "It is a beginning. Minor yes, but unless it is watched, each flicker stamped out—" He turned the cup in his fingers.

Piers said, "There will not be war."

"No, by Gad." The old man's head rattled. "There will not be war. We will not permit war again." His eyes were canny. "We are able to prevent it. We will send in our International troops. We will watch as we have watched in Germany these years." For him, the armed supervision of Germany was already in the past.

120

Piers spoke out in desperation. "Have you noticed what is behind these incidents?"

"I know," Evanhurst stated, omnipotent. "Those niggers ain't content with their Equatorial State. I knew they wouldn't be, I warned Anstruther. They want all of Africa. Africa for Africans. You've heard it? It strikes the memory, doesn't it? Years ago it was Asia for Asiatics. Do you remember or were you too young, my boy?"

"I was a combatant in the Last War."

"You do remember. They're driving now. These incidents, episodes if you like. Driving against South Africa. Infiltration can't work; you can spot a nigger. A war—that's better. There's more of them. The white birth rate falls, the niggers breed like germs, and since we've given them our medical science, nature doesn't take care of it the way it used to. Lebensraum. That's what they're after, the whole damn black continent." He fixed a wily eye. "We're too strong in the north for them, so they're heading south. But after they take the south—" He believed it. His brain had been diseased by Schern. It wasn't a man for a man; it was three men for Evanhurst, titular leader of peace if Anstruther were gone. And Anstruther was gone.

"The Germans are gentlemen like ourselves." That was Hugo von Eynar. Schern to whisper the poison. "After they take the south, the north. What price British prestige then?" Brecklein for vested interest. "We can build the planes you want if allowed, better planes. We have the knowledge, the material. We can assemble them, ship them, and they'll cost you less.

There is money to be made." Three men for Evan-hurst, none needed for Gordon, the woman had him. With Anstruther gone, no one else was important. The Germans knew that Anstruther was dead.

Piers said, without hope, "Have you noticed the names of those against whom the incidents have been said to occur? German all, Boer if you like or they claim Belgium, Holland. But German source."

A smile narrowed Evanhurst's mouth. "You saw that. Yes, it hasn't escaped me. Didn't think the Inter-national would care if they carved up a few Germans. Sly devils."

Even that contingency had been figured. The dou-ble cross doubled. The redouble. And what matter if a few German farm colonists were, as Evanhurst ex-pressed it, carved up? The human sacrifice for the Fatherland. The old, old glory. Without knowledge or permission of the sacrificed, the end without con-sideration of the means. The evil wisdom of Schern again rampant.

"They'll learn," the London secretary said and there was no humor on his face. "They'll learn, by Gad, a white man is a white man. No matter what his name."

"There is no color problem in International Peace," Piers quoted.

"If those bloody blacks choose to make one, they'll learn."

With lost hope, Piers asked, "Have you talked with Fabian?"

Evanhurst put the reed between his lips. "I've read his lying report. That's enough."

122

Piers said it then. "Secretary Anstruther has believed in Fabian."

Evanhurst's lips were tight over the cigarette. When he spoke it was as if he spoke of a man quite dead. "Anstruther wanted to believe in lasting peace. Belief tempered his judgment, Piers. You understand? A good man, Anstruther, perhaps too good for our realities."

Piers cried out, "Will you talk with Fabian?"

Evanhurst did not smile. "There is no reason to talk with Fabian."

Piers looked long at the old man, the ape. Determined that apedom should not be threatened. How could he be blind to Germany? She hadn't even bothered to change tactics in the years, the same scheme schemed over and again. She had not changed the names of these leaders. Schern, Brecklein, von Eynar. What good would it do to point out that Brecklein had been a high official in German production before and during the Last War? That Schern had been one of Nicolai's key men, of the inner secret circle? That Hugo von Eynar had commanded an air force over England, that Morgen von Eynar had been a spy?

They had answered this long ago to Evanhurst's complete satisfaction. Brecklein had worked with the Nazis, certainly; it was his only way to hold a segment of the capital class intact while awaiting deliverance from revolution. Schern had been a leader in espionage, yes; he had paid, five years' imprisonment. The book he wrote in prison, *The Blind Shall See,* the story of his regeneration, had been swallowed by wiser than this gullible ape. Von Eynar, who could deny any youth of those days being filled with patriotism for the defense of his country? A man who did not fight for his country then was less than a man. It was the Fatherland for which he had fought, not National Socialism. It was easy to forgive Hugo. Furthermore he was so gentleman, so tall, so fair, so charming.

And Morgen? Who would bother in peace to find excuses for Morgen after once looking upon her? Only a fool. Who knew she had been a spy save Piers Hunt? The others who had known were dead. Those who kissed did not live to tell. Accident alone that Piers lived.

Even if Evanhurst did not in his skeptical soul believe the disavowals of these men, he did not fear. This time Britain could handle Germany before she got out of hand. Piers asked, a young man deferring to an old, an undersecretary deferring to the second most important man in the Conclave; asked humbly knowing the answer, "What will be your vote, Lord Evanhurst? On the German matter."

The old man could smile now, on a protégé, on the grandson of an old and equal friend. "I shall vote for withdrawal. With a recommendation that the militia be sent into Equatorial Africa to observe matters there."

There was no need to remain longer. It was said. Piers left the apartment and returned to his room. He looked out at the city without seeing the towers, the spring burgeoning. He ticked them off. Anstruther, Gordon, Evanhurst. Germany was certain. She could afford arrogance to an undersecretary who dared raise his piping against entrenched power. The hopelessness in him was a goad. There could still be hope. If he could reach Fabian. He knew now he must reach Fabian. The black man must be made to see his personal peril, the peril to his land and race, if not the peril in which the world lay. No matter what lies Germany had fed Fabian, he, Piers, could expose them. Because he had Hugo's letters to back up his personal knowledge of the incidents.

He sat at the desk and he scrawled words, crossing out, emending. He read the satisfactory text: "David. Imperative. Will tell all of desert. Come again. Same place." He put no signature to it. A signature would give away what the salutation and message would not. If David saw it, or Fabian, they would understand. He copied it legibly in duplicate, addressed one envelope to *The New York Times,* another to the *Herald Tribune.* He enclosed money and a note. The personal was to run until Sunday. He signed his name, George Thompson. He took then the Hugo letters. They must not be risked until Fabian had seen them. He sealed them within an envelope, addressed it to safe-keeping. He dropped the envelopes into the mail chute before descending to the lobby.

He didn't notice Cassidy until he was outside the hotel, his hand lifted for a cab. He beckoned, "You might as well join me."

"Might as well," Cassidy said. He followed Piers into the cab, spoke, "Fifty-fourth street precinct house, Bud."

Piers said, "I'm on my way to the Peace offices."

"Captain Devlin wants to talk to you."

Piers put a cigarette in his mouth. It didn't matter.

Nothing mattered in this moment of bitterness, nothing but reaching Fabian in time. He could give Devlin some story, it wasn't important. He struck a match. "Did Captain Devlin put you on me?"

Cassidy rested his shapeless hat against the seat.

Piers vented some of his anger. "Don't tell me you're still keeping up the old gag that I'm not being tailed."

"You're being tailed all right," Cassidy agreed. "But Devlin would never have heard of it if that numbskull hadn't lost you last night. He was supposed to report to me but he got so rattled he went to his own precinct." He sighed heavily. "Then they get me out of bed and drag me down and we sort of get together on that briefcase. The one you lost."

The cab drew up at headquarters. Cassidy climbed out. "Do I pay for my own Maria?" Piers asked.

"Your cab, isn't it?"

Piers paid. None of this was Cassidy's fault. The guy hadn't even had his twenty-four hours' rest. Piers said, "For the record, your man didn't lose me. I stayed all night at the Plaza."

"With Lord Evanhurst?"

"Yeah," Piers said. Let him have the honor. Everything went back to Evanhurst, even Cassidy's lost sleep. He walked on past the old sergeant into the office. Devlin's face wasn't pleasant today. Piers sat down without suggestion. He started it, he himself wasn't pleasant, not now. "What do you want with me?"

"Just a little talk." The captain's heavy irony wasn't amusing. Devlin didn't know how unamusing he could be after Evanhurst. That was the amusing boy. Like that Italian in the long forgotten war Italy had waged on Ethiopia, giggling while he dropped his bombs. They were only niggers to him, too; funny how they scattered when destruction dived out of the sky. Funny, yes.

"About that briefcase you lost when you were Mr.—Henderson, wasn't it?" Devlin had the report under his hand, referred to it without need.

"What about it?" Piers demanded.

"Made of the best alligator—about so big, wasn't it? With play manuscripts in it." His voice was heavy. "Play manuscripts, yet." He spoke out hard now, "Where did you get that briefcase?"

Piers was patient, slowly patient. "I had it made for me at the Lake of the Crocodiles. That's in Africa, in case you aren't familiar with it. It was a good briefcase, the best. I'll admit it didn't have manuscripts in it. I wouldn't be at liberty to tell you what was in it. As for giving you the name Henderson, we of the Peace Commission must be careful not to receive publicity"—he waited long enough—"when on secret mission."

Devlin looked at Cassidy. Cassidy's lip stuck out. He said, "Could be."

"Could be, yes," Piers smiled. "Who put you on my tail, Cassidy?"

Cassidy rolled the words. "That I am not at liberty to dee-vulge, Mr. Hunt. Like you and your secret mission, maybe?"

"You prove different," Piers suggested. He turned on Devlin. "And now am I and my pet bulldog allowed to depart? De Witt Gordon is waiting for me at the Peace offices."

Devlin said, "What do you know of John Smith?"

"To which John Smith do you refer? The English adventurer or the—"

"You know damn well which John Smith I'm asking about." The man's face was discolored. "The guy that got bumped off by a taxicab when you lost your briefcase."

Piers didn't hesitate. "He was a little rat-toothed individual who traveled in the chair car up from Washington night before last. He was following me. He was following me to get his hands on a briefcase, made to order of the best alligator skin from the Lake of the Crocodiles. He thought it was Secretary Anstruther's case." He could go into truth now. "I presented the Secretary with one some years ago. I don't think you need ask why that Smith wanted the Secretary's briefcase. He was, as you doubtless know, a German."

If he told the whole truth, that his loss was but an invention to facilitate inquiries about John Smith—better this way. Better that he was on record as losing a case which no one, not even these cops, believed was his. It might call off the dogs long enough for David to come to him.

"Why would you be having Secretary Anstruther's case?" Cassidy asked.

Piers laughed a little. "The Secretary never parts with his. Evidently John Smith didn't know that. He must have believed that I, as the Foreign Undersecretary, carried it."

Devlin asked, "How did you know this guy was a German?"

Piers met his eye. "I didn't until I came here that day to report my loss. The officer outside mentioned John Smith might well have been Johann Schmidt. The uncle's accent." He leaned to the captain. "Do you have the uncle's name and address?"

Devlin put a tooth over the corner of his lip. "Phonies. We're looking for him." He asked gruffly but his voice begged reassurance, "We aren't going to have trouble with Germany again, are we? Some of the newspapers seem to think so. I was in the Last War. I don't ever want—"

"We are not going to have war again," Piers said somberly. He came to his feet. "May I go now? And must Cassidy come with me?"

Cassidy put his feet on the floor, pushed up heavily. "I got my orders, Hunt. I told you they weren't from Captain Devlin." But he wasn't unfriendly now. He didn't want war.

"And you can't tell me who or why?"

"I don't know, Hunt." He rubbed his cheek. "I don't know nothing about this case. You're to be followed. Maybe it's to be sure you don't get hurt. All I know is my orders come straight from the Commissioner himself. Follow you. That's all."

"And you're looking for the briefcase, too."

Cassidy said, "I already told you that."

Piers moved slowly. He said aloud, "I wonder what the Commissioner of Police would want with Anstruther's briefcase."

There had been traitors in the Last War, in high

places, men who played the enemy's game. This was peace. And how many without fear of stigma in time of peace, how many other than Evanhurst, were playing the German hand?

"Maybe he's wondering what you'd want with it," Cassidy said slowly.

Piers said, "That's the part I don't understand."

2.

The girl at the desk had hair by Gauguin and the manners of royalty. Her black satin was Chatin-Roux. She said, "You wish to see Secretary Gordon?" Her nose implied his inaccessibility.

"If you don't mind." Piers gave her equal hauteur. He could tell it didn't go over. "The name is Piers Hunt." His name wasn't known to her.

She spoke into a box on her desk. He walked away to a chair twisted of aluminum and cafe-au-lait leather. It was more comfortable than it appeared. The elegant young woman raised her voice one cultured notch. "His secretary will be out at once, Mr. Hunt." She seemed a little proud and not a little surprised at her prowess in obtaining the secretary. He didn't protest. He might as well go through Gordon's hoops as long as he was here.

The first secretary was a rarer edition of the girl at the desk save that her hair was cobalt and her mouth a deeper crimson. She sat in a chair beside Piers. "Mr. Hunt?" She held an envelope. "Mr. Gordon had to leave for Washington. The President summoned him. We tried to locate you but you'd left the hotel. Mr. Gordon asked me to give you this note." She offered the envelope.

He broke it open and read,

"My dear Piers—
The President sent for me this morning. He also wants to see you. Will you get down here as soon as possible? I've asked Miss Maybrick to see about a plane for you. Sorry not to wait but he was urgent and the hotel didn't know what time you'd return."

The President must have got on to something. And Gordon was there first. Piers' eye met Miss Maybrick's. She might have been reading the note over his shoulder. She said, "I've already ordered the plane to stand ready. One of our cars is waiting to take you to the port. Is that satisfactory?"

He put the note back into her hand. "Orders are orders." He didn't like flying with an unknown pilot, entering a prepared car, but there was nothing else to do. Gordon had had the head start.

"What time did Mr. Gordon take off?"

"About ten. It was nine-thirty when the President phoned. We called your hotel but your room didn't answer."

It was nearing one now. It would be mid-afternoon before he could reach Washington. By then it might be too late. If Gordon had known he was breakfasting with Evanhurst—he didn't know. He'd left the suite last night before the engagement was made. Cursing fate didn't change her megrims.

"I'm ready."

Miss Maybrick said, "Beulah, will you ring the car, please?" Beulah was the creation at the desk. She was frankly puzzled now. "Mr. Hunt will be down at once."

It couldn't be that the phony von Eynar letters had been discovered, that this was a plan to get him out of the way; not with Miss Maybrick and Beulah and all the New York branch of the Peace office in on it. He was the only one in the elevator. He asked, "What time does Nick Pulaski come on duty?"

"Six o'clock." The boy asked after two floors, "Nick a friend of yours?"

They reached the first floor lobby. "I am a friend of his," Piers said. He paused at the cigar counter, bought two bars of chocolate and a pack of cigarettes, the early editions of the afternoon papers. It would be better not to think on the two-hour run to Washington; certainly it would be discretion to refrain from unnecessary speech with Gordon's man. It didn't look as if he'd get any lunch. Lord Evanhurst's breakfast had fortunately been British-hearty.

The car thrummed at the curb, the International Peace insignia on the door, a small identifying round. Piers asked, "Airport?"

"Yes, sir." The chauffeur hadn't a face, only a chauffeur's mask, but he drove neatly and without time waste to LaGuardia Field. Not until the car stopped did Piers realize how tightly he'd held himself on the drive and how foolish were his fears at this time. Nothing was going to happen to him when he'd been summoned by the President of the United States. The Germans wouldn't be that hapless.

The pilot of the small cabin plane was American as Cape Cod. Piers settled himself with the papers, peeled a chocolate bar, and was lifted into the sky. The news sheets were on to Fabian at last. There was a photo of him from the first Conclave, dressed in his scarlet robes of state, the towering headgear reducing his face to a small dark blob. The great Fabian, the lines ran, man of mystery, leader of Equatorial Africa, has arrived by private plane from his homeland. There was no mention of where he was putting up.

There was no mention anywhere at all of Anstruther. That in itself was a warning. The State Department and the President must have learned something to substantiate rumor. The men who gave out Peace information to the papers had been muted. There was a bland interview with Brecklein quoting statistical figures of Germany's production, and the Fatherland's hope for increased productivity in the "golden era of the coming years." A Ward and Dunley photo went with the interview. Brecklein's pictured face was solid, prosperous, safe. No one would take notice of the thin lips, no one who had not faced the stone eyes above that mouth.

Piers put away the papers and ate his second chocolate bar. He remembered Cassidy all at once, half glanced over his shoulder amusedly for sight of a plane pursuing. Certainly Cassidy wouldn't be expected to follow to the White House doors. An interview with the President of the United States couldn't be suspect.

Piers didn't know the President. He'd seen the face and gestures in an occasional newsreel, heard the voice on screen and radio. The man was somewhat younger than Anstruther and Evanhurst's generation; he'd been coming up in politics during the Last War, too old to be caught in it, he'd done nothing controversial either then or in the peace decade. He was considered a good president, neither too precious nor too common for the people at large, some kind of farm background, westerly; he liked golf, fried chicken, fishing as a matter of course, and piloting his own plane. He'd strictly kept his hands off Anstruther and the Peace policies.

The pilot in his separate cubicle had had nothing to say on the flight. Realizing it suddenly, the cold sledge of suspicion struck at Piers' stomach. This could have been a ruse. He looked out the window; green country lay quilted below. He lifted the communication, asked, "About there?"

"Yeah."

Piers waited but the pilot had nothing more to say. Piers replaced the phone. It was ridiculous to fear. The Germans couldn't have infiltrated the Peace office. Gordon wasn't a traitor, no matter what his commitments. He had no reason to do away with Piers; he was an Anstruther man even as was Piers. And the President waited. One misadventure by plane could be swallowed but two would indubitably stick in the gullet. Whatever the President was not, he was more intelligent than that.

The communication sounded and he lifted it. "We're coming in now," the pilot said. "Look out and you'll see Washington monument. Looks like a lead pencil from here."

"Thanks." He looked out. They were circling Washington's marble whiteness and rich green. The plane landed quietly at the airport. There were two secret service men waiting. "Piers Hunt? The car's over this way."

"How did you know me without the carnation?" Piers asked.

The one on his right said, "You came down in Gordon's plane, didn't you?" It was Gordon who was known, the personalizing of the department.

The car was reassuring with its White House markings. There wasn't anything off color about this appointment then; the President had summoned him. And Gordon. Gordon who had got here first. Piers scowled a little and he lit a cigarette.

The secret service passed him into the White House by way of the porte-cochere. "The President is waiting for you in his private office." He followed them along the passageway to an unmarked door. One man entered; the other waited outside with him. Piers said, "Hot, isn't it?" The words were inane but less so than standing here silent like a political criminal.

The man wiped his neck.

The other returned. He held the door open. "Go right in, Mr. Hunt." Piers was inside then, without his escort, in the comfortable, historic study of the President of the United States. The President was standing behind his desk, his hand outstretched. "Delighted you could make it, Mr. Hunt." His handclasp was practicedly strong. "Draw up a chair. They're more comfortable than they look. We haven't streamlined the White House yet. Somehow one grows attached to the old things."

Piers felt as if he'd known the man for years, he was that like his newsreel and radio self. Gordon had risen from another of the chairs of old leather. Gordon, handsome, smiling, his dark suit fresh from a tailor's, his shoes glossy, his pores untouched by human sweat. Piers' summer-weight grays were more than crumpled; they smelled of Cassidy and the precinct house. His face needed a sponge.

Gordon said, "Thank God, you received the message, Piers. I tried to reach you early—"

"So your secretary told me." He was easy. "I was breakfasting with Lord Evanhurst."

Gordon wondered and the President said, "I understand you're an old friend of my friend, Lord Evanhurst. Cigarette?" But his social grace went from him when they were seated again. He said, "You know, of course, that Secretary Anstruther is missing?"

"Yes." Piers nodded. "Gordon told me Tuesday that he was overdue."

The President's face was sober. "I'm still too shocked over the news to know what to do. I only learned last night—"

Gordon spoke quickly. "I didn't want to tell you, sir. You have so many problems. I wanted to withhold it until we knew something definite, but—"

"I understand." His smile and Gordon's met, accepted each other. The President continued, "It's hard to have it happen at this time. So much depends on our present Conclave."

"Yes," Piers agreed.

"I've named Gordon Secretary pro tem." He said it as casually, with as little import as if he had named a village postmaster.

Because of the casualness it was a moment before Piers realized what had been said. His eyes leaped to Gordon and he gripped the arms of the chair to keep himself from rising. Gordon had the right expression, an acceptance of condition, enough humbleness, the will to do his best. The licking tongues of triumph were sublimated beneath that well-bred, well-barbered face. And Piers was silenced. He could not protest. He couldn't demand that he be named. Gordon was the logical man to succeed in so far as the President Ape knew. Certainly the sweating, soiled fellow who called himself Piers Hunt couldn't be selected to preside over the most important conclave of the decade.

Gordon had won this set. And Piers, knowing the smugness, certain of the decision beneath the superb facade, was forced to express "Congratulations" as if the word were not lye on his tongue. He knew then that had Gordon communicated with him this morning, he would have created delay for Piers in New York. He would have made certain that Piers did not accompany him to Washington. He had planned this well, informing the President last night, stepping into the wanted shoes this morning. Gordon said with that disarming smile, "I'm still hoping that I won't have a chance to accept the position, Mr. President." And he included Piers in the smile. "I'll hope until Sunday afternoon that Anstruther will return."

"You understand," the President's voice was troubled, "we are not releasing the fact that Secretary Anstruther is missing until after the Conclave." He frowned. "Some of the newspapermen will speculate —they have already—but we will say nothing until the opening on Sunday. At that time a small notice that due to illness—illness, you understand—Secretary Anstruther cannot as yet be present, that Secretary Gordon will preside pro tem in his place."

Piers said, "I won't divulge any further information."

The President nodded his approval. Gordon caught the undertone. It was in the faint drawing together of his brows.

"I understand the importance of secrecy." Piers' voice was a silken thread. That Gordon knew there was to be enmity was good. There was no other way to play it. Piers couldn't stab in the back.

The President's eyes gleamed. "Gordon tells me you were the last man to see Anstruther."

No stab in the back, not even if the other man had no such compunctions. "I saw him off in Alexandria, sir."

"Tell me about it."

He could have told it the same under scopolamin. But he welcomed the opportunity to put on high official record what must be recorded. The President was not accessible normally to such as he. He had learned that in Washington on Thursday when he had no congressman or senator or Gordon to act as inductor. He said simply, "I phoned the secretary in Berne. There had been another touch of border trouble— you've heard of the so-called incidents?"

The President nodded. Gordon opened his mouth but Piers didn't allow him sound. "They aren't important although certain nations for their own benefits and to the detriment of Equatorial Africa have tried to blow them up as such." He smiled at Gordon, imitating the man's open, winning facial contortion. It was a poor imitation but Gordon was uneasy. "I knew that if Anstruther could go over my reports, talk with the Africans whom I had, he would know this."

"You talked with Fabian?" Gordon suggested.

"No." It had been a deliberate attempt to discredit. Piers turned to the desk. "You may know, Mr. President, that it is difficult to have audience with Fabian, more so than with you for instance."

The President said, "I am always available at any time."

"I tried to see you Tuesday." He dropped it in passing. "It isn't that Fabian remains closeted in dignity; he is among his people except for state occasions. He believes this to be the wiser way of governing. He is leader of Equatorial Africa as well as Secretary of Peace, you know."

"A benevolent dictator," Gordon stated.

"No." Piers was sharp. That phrase had been in the Hugo letters, *a dictator, although benevolent.* "He decrees no law. All laws are made by the people." There must not be open conflict in this room. He turned back to the President. "Fabian, however, was available at any time to Anstruther. If Anstruther had felt the need of seeing Fabian, he could have done so. Anstruther is one of the few men in the world who actually has spoken with Fabian."

"Yes." The President's interest was titillated. "Secretary Anstruther has told me. He believes Fabian to be a great man."

"Yes." And Fabian had sent David with a gun. To take at gun point what the Germans too would take by force. "They are friends as well as leaders." He put a fresh cigarette in his mouth. "I'll make this brief, sir. I went into Africa when the first spot of trouble appeared. I saw with my own eyes what was causing it. The secretary and I went over my findings and he agreed with me that whereas the incidents themselves were doubtless unimportant, farm squabbles—Fabian had not even considered them worthy of international investigation—undeniably they were German-fomented."

Gordon's control was good. The President had disbelief unflexing his mouth. "Did you say German-fomented?"

"Yes, I did, sir. Undeniably. I can prove it. I have the facts if you wish to examine them. I'll have to send to Berne for them naturally. I didn't bring them along as I expected Anstruther to have his copies here. The proof was sufficient for Anstruther to state in no uncertain terms that he would make certain that Germany should remain under the protectorate for the prescribed years."

Gordon didn't like it at all. The President was fashioned of wonderment.

"The Secretary was ready to take the plane to Lisbon when a wire from Fabian, asking him to meet at the Lake of the Crocodiles, changed his plans. He thought it must be a new incident. There was a small plane leaving that day for the Equatorial border—the department doesn't have its own planes in Africa. I saw Anstruther off in it. He was perfectly well. There was no reason for me to feel uneasy and yet—after he left, I did. Call it that sixth sense. I made enquiries and learned that Gundar Abersohn had piloted the plane that day. The Arabian pilot had had a sudden stomach attack after breakfast. I've learned since, as I told Gordon, that Fabian could not possibly have sent the wire. He was in Tibet."

The President was a startled faun. He shook his head, kept shaking it as if it wouldn't stop. "What do you think has happened?" He knocked over a desk calendar feeling for his cigarette case.

Piers lifted his shoulders. "It's possible that the Germans didn't want Secretary Anstruther to attend the Conclave, sir."

"But that's kidnaping!"

"Or murder."

The head began to pendulum again. "Oh no. No. We're at peace with Germany. All the nations are at peace. Things like that don't happen today. In the Last War—"

"It isn't so far away." He couldn't keep the fear from his voice.

"No. No. But it's incredible, Hunt. This is the time of peace."

"The time for vigilance if we would continue peace. Those are Secretary Anstruther's words." They weren't but they had come from the spirit of Anstruther.

The President was moving his hands, the way a woman would, a woman in anguish. "What to do? We cannot accuse Germany. We cannot make trouble —you have proof?" He didn't want proof; proof meant trouble.

"I have facts."

"I'd like to see them," Gordon said bluntly.

Piers looked at him. "I will cable Nickerson tonight."

"We mustn't have trouble," the President reiterated. "It is just such things as these that are the roots of war. And without Anstruther—" The anguish bit his voice now. "You think Anstruther is dead?"

"I do not believe it would be safe otherwise. He could not be spirited away, not and be allowed to return and tell."

"Yes." He accepted the inevitable. His mouth was haggard. "You'll help, Gordon? In every way? To bring the Conclave off, and after—" The search for Anstruther must wait on peace. The Secretary would decree it so. But if Germany won her point, there would never be an avenger. The President leaned over his desk. "We must make certain that there is no leakage of our news, gentlemen." He said almost to himself, "I don't know what to do."

He was a busy man. The office outside was filled with appointments. Gordon and Piers were not shown out through that office from whence might come more rumors. They left through the private door under the escort again of the secret service. They were guided to a car in the drive. This had no official seal.

Piers asked, "Are we sharing the plane back?"

"I'm staying over." Gordon's face was important. "I'll have to visit the department tomorrow, see how things are going." He spoke to the man at the wheel. "Do you mind dropping me at the Mayflower before you take Mr. Hunt to the airport?" To Piers he said, "I keep an apartment there."

Piers said, "I'll hop off where you do."

Gordon's eyes moved doubtfully.

"There are some men I want to see. I might as well stop over. No use making a flight for just one of us."

"I don't know when I'll get away." It came quickly.

"It doesn't matter. I don't need a private plane. Take off whenever you like." He preferred a commercial ride, particularly now. "I'll go up on one of the regular runs when I finish my business."

Gordon spoke cautiously, "If you need any introductions—"

"I know the men I'm looking for." Piers didn't add to it.

The car left them at the door. Gordon didn't like Piers at his side entering the grandeur and glory of the corridor. Here important men and women met to settle affairs of state in private court. Here unimportant men in dirty linen didn't belong. Particularly not at the side of the new Secretary of Peace, De Witt Gordon.

Piers was definitely surprised when Gordon said, "Come up and have a drink with me before we separate." Surprise was underlined with doubt. He had expected Gordon to eliminate him with a nod at the elevators. Curiosity at the change of attitude made him accept the offer, and he entered the gilt elevator behind the new secretary.

The rooms were a suite, a handsome, expensive setting. The decor was white and ivy green, there were good original oils, even a small Renoir on the walls. Piers sat hesitantly on the whiteness of a chair. "Your own things?"

"Yes." Gordon was at the plastic bar. "I'm here most of the year. Hotel stuff is too depressing."

Salary couldn't cover it, nor could Gordon's undistinguished background afford sufficient inheritance. It had never occurred to Piers before. There were ways to make money even in the Peace Department if you knew the right men, the brilliant investments: Spanish liquors, English shipping, Russian exports, American airlanes, German production. Each country would offer some means. Gordon was doubtless a rich man, and a rich man didn't have a selling price. Gordon wouldn't need to sell out peace. Morgen had been necessary.

Gordon brought the glass, crystal sheer as water, silver embossed monogram. "I didn't ask. It's Napoleon—" He sat down on the couch opposite.

Piers tasted. It was right.

Gordon drank again and when he set down the glass it rang against the metal table like a temple bell. He spoke quietly but distinctly. "I want you to give me Secretary Anstruther's papers."

3.

Piers didn't attempt to answer at once. He drank from the glass again, drank without moving his eyes from his opponent. When he put down his glass it was without sound. He said, "I don't have them."

Gordon wasn't annoyed; he had expected this parry. He reasoned as with a child, "Come, Piers. It's undeniable that you had his briefcase at the Alexandria airport. That's been proven without a doubt."

"By Schern's spies," Piers bit out.

Gordon flushed slightly. "And by the English inspectors," he countered. "I won't say you know more than you've told about what has happened to the old man—"

Piers broke in angrily, "Are you suggesting that I had a—"

Gordon's voice was an iron door. "I repeat that I won't say you're withholding information. But there isn't any doubt that you had his case in your possession after he left the port. I want his papers."

Piers lifted his glass. "I don't have them." His mouth was sullen.

"Listen, Piers," Gordon's choler was rising. "As acting head of the Peace Department those papers belong in my hands."

Piers drank.

"What purpose have you in hiding them? Don't you want to further international peace?"

"You're calling me a liar," Piers warned. He put down his glass again.

"I don't want to call you a liar," Gordon placated. He would recall the adages, molasses preferable to vinegar, all of them save the important one of seating himself above the salt. "But what else do you expect me to say? You lied to me about Anstruther leaving for Lisbon. I know the briefcase was in your possession. I know it contained his most important papers—he cabled me he was carrying them with him, too important to trust to the air mails. Yet you deny having them."

"I told you it was my briefcase. Resemblance."

"Yours wasn't lettered with the old man's monogram, was it?" Gordon asked with malice.

Gordon even knew that. Faded gold lettering by the hasp. But English inspectors and German spies hadn't based their knowledge on three scarred letters. They knew he had had the briefcase because they knew how it came into his possession. Gordon wouldn't mention that. Ten to one they hadn't told him that part of it. Piers smiled. Not even Schern's spies of highest intelligence knew for certain that Anstruther wouldn't reappear. They hadn't any of them had a report on the death of Anstruther. Even Fabian's men didn't know how he had died.

Gordon said, "I see no reason to quarrel. You have been a valuable man to our Peace Department."

He caught the inflection. That would be the next move. He had known it.

"We're after the same thing. Peace," Gordon appeased. "What I'm asking is certainly reasonable. If the old man gave you those papers to carry across, knowing he was on a dangerous mission; if he told you to guard them in utmost secrecy, I can understand. But he couldn't foresee what has happened. As matters now stand, I must have the papers. I can't conduct the Conclave as Anstruther would wish it conducted unless I know his wishes in the matter. You can understand that."

He could understand that. It was reasonable; it was smooth, well-oiled from every approach. And if Morgen, and bulwarking her Brecklein and Schern, were not behind Gordon's shoulders, Piers would capitulate. But he knew that papers could disappear; he knew they could be doctored. He said, "I told the President what Anstruther's opinion is. If you doubt it you will see my notes when Nickerson sends them."

"Your notes, not Anstruther's."

Piers stood and felt for his hat. He looked down at Gordon, as if Gordon were far below him in a chasm. "I'll tell you what I want," he said softly. "I want to make the initial speech at the Conclave. Let me do that and I'll get you anything you want."

Gordon was sharpened to anger. He pushed up from the couch and his fist was knotted at his side. "I'm not making any trades," he stated. And then the realization of his position as against that of Piers steadied him; sureness filled him, his fingers loosed. His voice was strong. And it was cold. "As presiding officer of the Conclave, I naturally must make the keynote address." He was in, Piers out; there was no reason for generosity. "As Secretary, I do not need to trade with you. All Peace Department material, including yours, belongs in my hands. I can force you to turn it over to me. Good day, Piers."

It was no idle threat; it was certainty. Piers went out, rang for the elevator. He was sticky with heat. The brandy on an empty stomach didn't help. Napoleon brandy hadn't been tasted outside Germany since the days of the occupation of Paris. Gordon had attentive friends. The elevator man's peaked face was startled at a man laughing aloud in his loneness. The cage whirred to the main floor. Laughter was shaking Piers' stomach silently. Gordon couldn't lay hands on those papers for his dear friends, not for all the brandy that had been stolen from France. Nor could the dear friends turn the papers over to Gordon. They were as safe as if they'd been buried in the Nubian grave.

The difficulty was that open rupture would mean redoubling of surveillance. He wasn't quite sure how he could safely, first retrieve and then transport the memoranda to the opening of the Conclave on Sunday. It would be chancey. Would Gordon dare dismiss him from the department? If the breach widened he would, and he'd have his neat packet of cause for the President. Refusal to cooperate with the department, hostility to the cause of peace—the lies would contain enough truth to pass muster. It would be one sure way to silence Piers in Conclave.

Gordon hadn't carried the briefcase tale as yet to the President. And why? Because he wanted to get the papers first, to make sure that nothing inimical to the furtherance of his career was disclosed. Because Morgen had asked for them? Gordon was no mean opponent; he was wiser in the wrongs of diplomacy than his generation. Would he include suspicion of murder in his accusation? Piers scowled himself into a phone booth. Gordon had definitely hinted at that. With it spoken out, he would have no trouble getting rid of Piers for good and all. He didn't need that weapon. He could discredit Piers without going that far. For the first time it occurred to Piers that it might have been Gordon who put Cassidy on him.

He looked up the number of the British Embassy, dropped the coin and dialed. He asked for Herbert Watkins or where to find him. Watkins himself came to the phone.

"This is Piers Hunt."

Watkins expressed surprise. "Where are you?"

"The Mayflower. Can you have dinner with me?" Watkins hesitated.

Piers said, "I think it's important, Bert. I've only tonight. Back to New York in the morning. I don't know if I'll get down again." He didn't know if he would be alive tomorrow. Even now his trail might have been freshened, one of those well-dressed men outside could wear the colors of Brecklein or Fabian or—or Gordon. He had once seen a man in Paris walk out of a phone booth into the extinction of a bullet. The hairs rose on the back of his head, something of urgency went into his demand. "Well?"

Watkins said, still with faint hesitancy, "I'll meet you. There?"

He didn't want to remain here in Gordon's terri-

tory; he was afraid to take a chance on going else-
where. He answered finally, "Yes. I'll be in the bar."

"Be around shortly."

Piers hung up. He pushed his hat forward, looking
through the pane. A man was waiting for the booth.
Piers opened the door, stepped forth without bravery.
He held himself stiff, moving wooden legs down the
elegance of corridor, found the bar. He took a stool
that placed his back to the wall, his eyes to the door.
There were glances at him, some curious, too many
nose-lifted. He realized again his distinct shoddiness.
One thing certain, he didn't look important enough
to be marked for death. Neither had John Smith.

Even the barman had his nose wrinkled. Piers said,
"Brandy." slung a ten-dollar bill on the bar and was
sorry. Why should he give a tinker's damn about the
barman's snobbery or that of his customers? He swallowed from the glass and his stomach burned. He'd
had enough brandy; what he needed was food. Until
Watkins arrived, he'd have to husband this drink,
despite the disapproval of the barman. Watkins was
long. He reluctantly ordered a second drink, sipped
at it. When he saw the Englishman in the doorway, he
stood to signal and felt his head twirl. He kept his
hand flat on the bar while the man advanced, stolid
and reassuring, neat in his blue serge, the weathered
face below the bristled, graying head curious.

Piers sank to the stool again. "Have a drink, Bert?"
His voice seemed to waver.

"Yes." Watkins sat next him but he was dubious.

Piers said, "I'm glad you could come. I won't take
another. I haven't eaten since breakfast."

"Let's eat now."

"Have your drink first. Do you know a place we can go? I don't know Washington well. I'd rather not stay here. I want to talk without Gordon hearing." He knew he was saying too much but his voice ran on in spite of himself. "The way you hesitated about coming I thought maybe you'd been warned already to stay away from me."

"For God's sake," Watkins breathed and sympathy came over his square face. "Bad as that, is it? I was supposed to be on tap for a call from the Lud and a state dinner. I slipped out."

"You're a friend," Piers said dreamily. He wanted to put his head on the cool silvery bar and sleep.

Watkins downed his drink, took Piers' arm. "We'll eat now, old man."

Piers' legs were brittle. He let the Briton guide him. He repeated, "You're a friend, Bert. I'll be all right when I've had some food. I hadn't a chance to eat today. I've been with the President—fancy that!—and *Secretary* Gordon." He felt Watkins' fingers tighten. "Fancy that, too!" They were outside in the mildness of night. He saw the curious passersby in a blur. He drew back as the taxi rolled up to the curb. "You're going to take a cab?"

"Too far to walk."

He hadn't the strength to resist. Watkins pushed him in, gave an address. "We're going to my digs, Piers. We can talk there."

"He could have put something in the brandy," Piers said through the dream.

"Who?" Watkins was sharp.

"*Secretary* Gordon. I didn't think of it before. I hardly believe he would—yet. But he could have." And he could have appeared, opportune, regretful for an employee under liquor. He could have moved Piers to his room, the kind Gordon, the great Gordon. There'd be no further need for surveillance in German hands. Such a small favor delivering him to Schern—to force the papers. Or—it wouldn't matter about the papers if Piers were dead. No, they wouldn't kill, not yet, not until they knew the whereabouts of Anstruther.

They were at another hotel. He couldn't distinguish the name but Watkins' hand was firm. The elevator crept. And then he was in a hotel room, nothing of grandeur, just a room. Watkins urging, "Don't lie down there. Get under the shower, cold." And Watkins speaking into the phone while Piers wavered to the bath, "Send up two of the biggest steaks in the kitchen. All that goes with it. Plenty of strong coffee."

Piers let the cold water smash at him. He wasn't so sleepy when he came out but his head was still light.

Watkins asked, "Better?"

"Yes, thanks. I need food."

"It's coming. What were you saying about Gordon —*Secretary* Gordon?"

Piers put on the dirty suit again. No wonder the glances of the men on the street had been strange. The substantial Watkins upholding a man in a grimy gray suit.

"Yes."

"Anstruther isn't coming back?"

"Did I say that?" His eyes focused hard now. "It

must be between us, Bertie. I can trust you as before?"

"Yes." Watkins' mouth was tight. "God help us, yes."

"How much do you know?"

"Anstruther's missing. That's no secret. Evanhurst is keeping me holed here just to listen in, to get word to him fast. Any crumb."

"I've given you a loaf."

"Don't worry. Tell me what's happened."

He couldn't tell Watkins all despite his trust. "No one knows. He hasn't been heard from. Since he left Alex."

"And you saw him off."

"You know that." He spoke wearily. "Everyone knows that. It ends right there."

"And Gordon?"

"He's Secretary. This afternoon. By official decree. It won't be announced until the Conclave opens."

Watkins repeated his prayer. "God help us."

"You know Gordon?"

"He's Evanhurst's delight. An example to us duds." He broke off. "There's food."

The waiter wheeled in the table. The scent of the meat made Piers' head turn faster.

"Don't get up," Watkins said. "We'll put it there."

The waiter fixed the table in front of Piers, uncovered dishes.

Watkins said, "We'll manage the rest." He shut the man from the room, pulled up a chair and seated himself across. "Eat now. Don't talk until you've eaten."

Piers wolfed at the food. He felt better at once. If

Gordon had tried to put him out, the dinner was counteracting the drug.

"How did it happen to be Gordon?"

"Who else? The President didn't know me; he doesn't know I'd have been Anstruther's choice. Gordon got there first. Not that it would have made any difference."

"You know where Gordon stands?"

"Yes."

"There's no doubt?"

"None at all." He thought of Morgen's flesh. "None at all."

Watkins lifted his coffee cup.

"I'm not beaten yet," Piers said. "I'm whipped but I'm not beaten. I won't be."

"You can't be. There's so few of us to stand for peace."

Piers hesitated. "You'd be named if anything happened to Evanhurst?"

Watkins was motionless. "Yes."

"He's an old man. Something could happen."

"These opportune events do not often occur." Watkins scooped a spoon of ice cream.

"Something could happen to him," Piers repeated stubbornly.

For a moment nothing changed, then the man's face turned dusty. The spoon clanged to the table. He shook a fierce head. "No. No. Nothing like that."

"I'm not suggesting death, Bert," Piers told him quickly. "But if he could be prevented from attending the Conclave—"

"You're drunk," Watkins said.

154

"Not now. A recall to London. A mission to India."

"He checks too carefully."

"A slight sickness," Piers persisted. "A stomach attack. A cold—"

There was no expression on Watkins' face while he thought about it. He made decision. "No. I couldn't be a party to it, Piers. I've worked my way up to the place I hold in International Peace. I've worked against plenty of odds—with him at the top, there's always plenty. But I've kept the peace. Some day I'll have his place and be able to carry on as I want. Until then I'll keep plodding. I'm a man of peace. I can't deny peace."

Piers accepted the finality but he accused, "You won't deny peace but you'll let the Germans take it away from you."

"I don't believe they can."

"You don't? With Evanhurst and Gordon as lead sheep? Who do you think can stop the withdrawal? Poor old Mancianargo? Dessaye? The Asiatics have their own problems, all they'll do is cast a courtesy vote with Britain and America. Even Fabian's on their side. Who is going to speak for peace?"

"The people."

He too had once had eternal faith in the people. But that was when the people had had a leader, when Anstruther had given them voice. "The people." Piers shook his head. "Give them bright pretty peace and they'll take peace. Give them war all dressed up in shiny slogans and they'll take war. You can't count on the people."

"The people didn't want the Last War, Piers.

There was never any spirit for it, not even in its necessity. Not in any country. You can't give the people another war. They are through with war."

"God knows I hope you're right," Piers said without hope. "But they haven't a voice."

"They will be heard." Watkins passed his cigarettes. "What's this about Fabian going over?"

"I don't know. He sent a man to talk with me at gunpoint the other night. Schern's men are after me too, and there's New York detectives."

Watkins frowned.

"They're all after Anstruther's papers. I'm supposed to have them."

Watkins caught at a hope. "You do?"

"I don't."

"But, Piers—"

Let suspicion tweak Watkins' eyebrows. He was too tired to care. "If I could speak to Fabian, then I'd believe we could beat the Germans."

"You could try. He knows Anstruther gave you his trust."

"I've been refused." He put his hand to his head. "I haven't been accused of murder yet. It will come."

"Anstruther is dead," Watkins said somberly.

"No one knows." He spoke out of passion. "Only two things have counted with me in twelve years, Bert. Anstruther and peace. I won't watch peace go too." He said, "Will you ride with me to the airport? I'm afraid to be alone tonight."

"Stay over with me."

He shook his head. "I must go back." David might come tonight. "Fabian's there. I keep hoping. Maybe he'll realize I can help him. And the Germans. Maybe I can beat them yet. Alone."

Watkins' face was sad. "I can't go along with you on violent means. I can't betray peace."

"I understand. Only I know better. We'll have to fight for peace this time. The apes are getting strong again." He put his hand in Watkins'. "Whatever you may hear of me between now and the Conclave, withhold judgment. I don't know how I'll have to play it from here on out. Just believe that whatever I do or say will be for one thing—peace in the world."

Watkins' clasp was strong. Stronger than his own.

VI

It wasn't midnight when he entered the Astor Bar.
They were there waiting for him. He hadn't expected
them to be here tonight; they should be celebrating
their victory in a more fitting way than a casual drink.
But they couldn't celebrate properly without the
skull of their enemy for a cup. The witchery of Morgen's face, the curve of her arm beckoned him. He
wanted to turn on his heel but he dare not. He
couldn't admit to them his defeat without admitting
to himself his despair. He pushed himself to the table
and stood above them.

Hugo rose insolently, Brecklein with fat reluctance.
Bianca's cold young face was watching something far
away. Piers' eyes traveled over Morgen, her throat, the
rose-red stuff folded over her shoulders and breast.
He said, "You've been on my mind all evening, Frau
General Schern."

"Brecklein," Hugo's voice was flat.

"My mistake." He sat down in Brecklein's chair
and he laid his hand on Morgen's arm.

She said, "Did Gordon return with you?"

They knew as he had known that they knew. They

knew where he had been this day. They knew what
the outcome must have been. He said, "No. He had
business that held him. Excellent brandy, Gordon
has." His lips twisted. "Drinking brandy with Gordon, I thought of you."

Brecklein asked dubiously, "Gordon remained in
Washington?"

"Yes." He craned up, scowling. "Get a chair. I
can't talk to you up there." He moved his finger over
Morgen's flesh. "You're warm," he said.

Brecklein managed a chair. "Gordon did not say
how long he would remain in Washington?"

Gordon hadn't communicated with them as yet.
They didn't know the deal had been consummated.
They wouldn't know from him. He said, "Gordon
sent no messages, Herr Brecklein." He hated the
touch of her. She burned like acid into the bones of
his fingers. "I'll have a brandy. A pity there is no
Napoleon."

Morgen said, "Witt asked us to meet him here."

"Important business." He shut out the others. "Do
you remember, Morgen,—the snow and the shell of
the Adlon? We found champagne, iced by winter. Do
you remember that night, Liebchen?"

Her eyes were wary, perhaps her mouth curved
remembrance but he couldn't know. He put his el-
bows on the table and he leaned himself to the frozen
young girl across from him. "You don't remember the
war, Bianca, do you? You were too young to know it."
He forced her hostile face to notice. "And the bombs
didn't drop over here, tearing to pieces children and
women and the old men. Like mad dogs, chewing up

human flesh and spewing it out on rotten earth. War is only a word to you, an outmoded word like feudalism and plague and slavery. You don't believe in it any more than you believe in those forgotten evils."

Morgen warned, "The war has been over for many years."

"I keep forgetting." He came back to the table, turned his head slowly to see her. "You were the most beautiful thing I'd ever known, Morgen." He touched the gossamer of her shoulders. "You wore an old shawl, do you remember? We met during that raid. You were wandering, lost, and so was I. Two lost babes in the broken Adlon."

"It has been rebuilt," Brecklein inserted with ponderous pride. His red face glistened from recall of the past, he wiped excrescence with the finest linen from Belgium. "Most modern. The rehabilitation of Berlin has been astounding to all who have seen."

"Piers has seen," Morgen said impatiently. "He's been in Berlin since the war."

They knew that. Not from a casual remark from someone he'd bumped into there. It wouldn't be from that.

"You know?" Brecklein said. "Astounding, is it not?"

"Astounding indeed," Piers bowed. "Germany is a remarkable country."

Morgen watched, uneasy, because he had forgotten stability and might forget again. Hugo watched, uneasy, because he didn't want Bianca to be disenchanted, or even Brecklein to know too much.

Piers lifted his glass. "I should toast Germany, that remarkable nation." The liquid spilled as he set it down untasted. And he saw by the door the familiar watching face of Cassidy. He called out, "There's Cassidy." His hand signaled. "Hugo, you must invite Cassidy over for a drink." If Cassidy came, saw their faces, the detective would know. And the chill that covered Piers here at this table would be thawed, he would be warm again. He called out, "Cassidy, there! The old elephant in the doorway, Hugo. He's my private bodyguard, you know." He shouted, "Cassidy!"

The detective had to come, to quiet him. He lumbered over but he wasn't pleased. "So you're back?"

"Safe and sound, if not tidy. Did you miss me? Or were you with me? To the very door of the White House. You will join my friends for a drink? Allow me to present Frau *General* Brecklein. Her husband, Herr *General* Brecklein. And her beloved brother, Hugo *General* von Eynar." Their hostility closed round him. But he wasn't afraid with Cassidy planted there. "All of Germany's Peace Commission. You didn't know Germany too had a Peace Commission? And this young lady is Miss Bianca Anstruther. You remember Secretary Anstruther?"

Cassidy mumbled, and added ill-at-ease, "No drink for me. I'm on duty." He lumbered away.

"He doesn't like the company I choose." Piers spoke lightly and the bitterness in Bianca's face was only a shadow of the bitterness enveloping him. "None the less I choose my own company. Morgen, the maid of Adlon; Morgen, the fay; Morgen, the—"

Bianca spoke sharply. "Hugo, take me home." Disgust blanched her face.

"You mustn't mind me," Piers said gently. He drained his glass watching Bianca and Hugo confer in undertone. He said, "No. I'm leaving. I might say too much if I remained here." He spoke softly: *"There is now no man alive to whom I dare speak my heart. I know, in truth, that it is a noble thing for man to fetter his feelings, to guard his tongue, whatever he may think."*

Morgen's hair was against his cheek. His words were for her ear alone. "Tomorrow noon, the Plaza. Alone. Important."

She shook her head.

"There are some things you'd like to know—" He looked into her eyes, her candid, sea-blue eyes.

She gave unwilling assent, fearing the trap. She herself had set too many.

"Good night." He lounged to the door, catching a glimpse of their huddle as he left the room. Swine and one small misguided pearl. He marched blindly to the news counter and stepped on a pair of tired black shoes.

Cassidy said, "I didn't think you'd be drinking with Heinies." His face sweated disgust.

Piers just looked at him. "We're all one big happy family. Haven't you heard of peace?"

"That's not what you were saying this morning."

He took the papers. "Skip it. I'm not the spokesman for peace any more." He went up wearily to his room. David wasn't there. The neon lights blinked patches on the floor. He took off the dirty suit, kicked it in a heap on the rug. He didn't want to see it again. He probably wouldn't, not for a long time. He doubted if he'd be here much longer. As soon as Gordon could unwind some red tape.

He wondered if Gordon had cabled Nickerson. There wasn't anything worth sending for; Piers didn't keep important notes in the office. He showered, shaved, laid out his things for morning. His room had been searched again. It didn't matter. He'd have to be at the Plaza before noon. He didn't know what would come next; he only knew it wouldn't be good. The main thing was to remain out of custody. The main thing was to keep alive. They wouldn't kill him —yet.

He read the papers for an hour or more before turning to sleep. It was as he knew it would be when the light was out and Broadway flickered now dark, now bright against his eyes. The old sickness again, the linger of her arm against his forefinger, the odor of her yellow hair, the promise of her voice. He had to play it this way. It was his only hope of breaking Gordon.

2.

He left the hotel before eleven, followed by Cassidy and a moon-faced man who read license plates. And doubtless somewhere beyond them by a dark man of the bush. He lost the first two in Times Square, the old last-man-on-the-subway trick. It took time but it was worth it. He didn't know if he'd lost the bush tracker. He rode as far as 72nd for safety, took a downtown train to Columbus Circle and walked across town to the Plaza. He wouldn't go up to his room; he must not be closeted with her. That agony could be avoided. He went to the desk, asked that he be paged on a call. When he turned she was just entering the lobby. She was in navy with ruff of white, and when she saw him her face lighted as if some flame leaped within her. He set his guts against her. He wouldn't be the victim this time.

He said, "I'm a little surprised that you came."

"You asked me to come." Her eyes were dark as sapphire.

He put his hand under her arm. "We won't lunch here. I've just avoided my bulldog and the mongrel at his heels. I don't want them around us." He steered her out of the hotel and into a cab. She sat there quiet, waiting. He said, "You are the loveliest thing I ever saw."

"That isn't why you asked me to come."

He leaned to the driver. "When there's no cab following get us to Seventy-ninth and Amsterdam. But be certain."

The cabbie saw a horned husband. He winked in his mirror.

"There's an old hotel, an aunt of mine once lived there. It'll be quiet at this hour."

She said nothing.

The cab ran a couple of red lights on Columbus. After that it cruised to the directed corner. "You're safe, Mister."

Piers matched the face and identification. Another Pole, Willie something. Could be Nick Pulaski's brother-in-law. He added an extra bill to the charge. "If you're around here in a couple of hours, we don't want to walk downtown."

"Keep your eyes open." The cabbie winked again.

Piers opened the street door into the cool, fumed oak tap-room, unchanged in the years upon years. There were two aging women in one booth with a coal-colored French poodle. The poodle had his own plate. A casual was at the bar. Piers sat across from Morgen in a sheltered corner, suggested from the menu, gave the orders. They sat in silence, measuring each other until the food was placed.

She spoke slowly, "What was the meaning of your act last night?"

He said, "It wasn't an act."

Her eyes would haunt him always. She'd learned to put sadness into them. "It wasn't real. The other night, your hatred, that was real."

He had to play it carefully. She was wise, as wise as she was beautiful, as beautiful as bad. "Yes, that was real," he admitted. "I hate your guts." He watched her flinch and he savored it. "But there's the reverse side of it. You know that one too, don't you? I thought I was finished with you twelve years ago. I've spent twelve years making certain I was through. And then you came. A man can hate—and want."

"You want me?"

"More than anything in the world." It rang true; it was true. That the denial of that want was stronger, she wouldn't know. Not yet.

Her lashes curved like shadows. "I am married to Caesar."

"And there's Gordon," he said.

She was alert. "He is a friend of Hugo's. And of mine. We met him at Rio, several years ago."

"You and Hugo?"

She was defensive. "Ernst was there on business. Hugo helped me pass the time." Her words came with difficulty. "Why didn't you return that night?"

"The war is long ago," he jeered.

"I waited for you."

"In Hugo's arms."

Her hand touched her cheek as if he had struck her.

"I came too soon." His voice was ugly. "I was headstrong that way. You remember?"

She was guarding her face but her sadness looked out of it. "When did you come?"

"That afternoon. I'd made a frightening discovery. I'd learned that your Brother Hugo wasn't one of us, that he was only posing as one. He belonged to Schern's inner secret circle." He shrugged. "I thought he was the key that you and I had been seeking."

She didn't move.

"I came rushing to tell you, to save you."

She said, "Yes."

He didn't have to go on; it was flagellation. "Yes. Hugo was with you. You didn't dream I'd take the chance of coming by day. You'd warned me so starkly of the risks. Risk didn't matter when it came to saving you. Hugo was with you. And he wasn't your brother. You were laughing." His ears were tortured again by the intimacy of laughter. "You were speaking without fear. I'd found what I was after."

She began to fork her food again. "Afterwards—

why didn't you give me over to the International Court to be tried for war guilt?"

He waited long until she looked at him. "Because I couldn't bear that you should die."

She met his face now. "I loved you. That was why you didn't die."

"I didn't die because I got out fast. In a way that even you and Schern hadn't heard about." He began to eat as if eating mattered.

"You were to have been executed long before that. We didn't need you. We had your information. I created delays. While you were listening, while I was lying to Hugo, I was plotting your escape. I was going with you as we had planned." That terrible honesty in which there was nothing but lies. "You don't believe that, Piers."

He said, "Let's remember it's all over, long ago. You're here. I'm here. There's no war. We disagree as to what the Peace Conclave should decide but it doesn't matter much."

She cried, "You must believe me. I've willed that you should know. After the war I waited for you to speak—or to return—"

"Then you married Brecklein. I thought it would be Schern. More important. But then he was imprisoned for five years, wasn't he? And Brecklein's a millionaire."

Pallor darkened her eyes. "I married Ernst only three years ago."

He didn't apologize. He said, "You shouldn't waste your time on me. I'm not important. You know now why Gordon stayed on in Washington."

She hesitated. Her hand moved. "Yes. He called me, after I returned to the hotel last night. Secretary Anstruther is missing." She added quickly, "No one is to know."

"I don't think it was news to you. You have Gordon. He'll stand up. You don't have to be nice to me. But you can answer one question. How important is Gordon to you?"

The surprise of the question lifted her face. "What do you mean?"

"I don't like Gordon." His eyes were blank. "I don't like him at all. I don't like him inheriting the position. It should have been mine."

"Yes. It should have been yours." She searched his face for cause, for treachery, for honesty. She saw only the shell of a face; nothing else was there. "What is it you want?"

He said, "What price Gordon?"

She took her time, silent while he lighted her cigarette and his own. She said then, "The Anstruther papers."

He broke the match in his fingers. She had said what he willed her to say; she had spoken. He began gently, "You know me better than that, Morgen."

"You asked that I bid." Her eyes were upon him, unflinching, unmoving.

He shook his head. "Without the papers, what would the Secretaryship avail me?"

Her voice whipped. "Have you that little faith in your own power? Why would you need the papers if you were Secretary?"

He spoke after pause. "I've never sold out to an enemy."

Her voice was quiet. "It is better to have a price, than to die."

He set each half of the broken match carefully on the oaken shield that lay between the woman and himself. The words came slowly. "You believe I am to die?"

She was silent.

"Like Anstruther." The smile hurt his mouth. "You are not the only ones who want the papers, you know. Gordon needs them badly." He kept smiling. "I know, if he doesn't, that he'll never lay eyes on them if his dear friends get in first. His price might be better. All of your heads. That might be as good as his head." He touched the table. "And he isn't the only one. Fabian wants those papers. I daresay Evanhurst would like them. Even the New York Police Department wants them."

She said with certainty, "But not one other can give you Anstruther's place. The position you should have had, that you intended to have."

He set his face. "What proof can you give me? Unless I see Gordon's head on the platter I wouldn't close any deal with you and your friends. I'd have to know it was certain."

Her lips moved with something like scorn. "You will sell out for that?"

" 'O, Opportunity, thy guilt is great!' " he repeated softly. "Every man has his price just as every woman makes mouths in a glass. That was said long ago. And I tried to tell it to you on Sunday night."

She was rigid. "It is well for you that you lowered the price."

"Gordon might think I'd upped it." His eyebrows slanted. "I want a meeting with all of you, Gordon present. I want confirmation before I sell."

"I'll tell Schern."

"And Hugo."

She gathered her gloves, her navy purse. "I shall tell Hugo."

"Tomorrow is Sunday."

She understood. "Tonight. The Waldorf. Late, say midnight."

"The witching hour." His lips curved without mirth. "A trap won't work. Cassidy will be behind me, you know. There's no good Schern thinking he'll take the papers without paying my price. No matter how many fat-bellied men and small rats with decayed teeth he sends after me. And you might mention, if I die, no one of you, nor Gordon, will ever lay hands on those papers."

They met face to face, each leaving the opposite oaken bench. He said, "Morgen——" and he put his arms around her and his mouth on hers. They held each other and no one cared. The old women cared only for the black poodle, the man at the bar only for his glass, the attendants only to be at rest. They held each other as alone, as undisturbed, as once they had been in the burning fragments of Berlin. They parted as simply as they had come together.

She pushed the hair from her cheek. "Don't play at love, Piers."

"I'm not playing that it's love." He moved at her

side. "I may have to go underground at any time. If I do I'll somehow manage to get to you." He opened the door and they left the old and cool room for the heat of the pavement. "There's our driver."

The cabbie was parked outside, his head on his shoulder, the radio singing. He opened the door for them. "Where to?"

Piers turned to her.

"It doesn't matter," she said. She had wrapped a dream about her. "The Metropolitan," she decided.

"Museum?" The driver's nose puzzled.

"Please."

Piers nodded. He didn't touch her. He knew too well how this could all be part of the evil charm.

He laughed. "I'm glad you came today, Morgen."

She spoke under her breath. "Why?"

His jaw was set. "Gordon's out to get me. I'm going to get him first."

The driver took the transverse across the park, circled to the Museum. He had muted his radio as if he sensed a wrongness in song at this time. Piers helped her to the walk. They didn't touch hands.

She said, "When you were young I knew ruthlessness was a part of you. Peace hasn't changed that. You must be careful. There are others as ruthless as you and more desperate."

He threw back his head and laughed out loud. "I'm not afraid." And the sun on his bared head turned chill as he watched the music of her walk up the steps, through the tall doors. He watched her vanish and the chill encompassed him. He knew with a sudden prescience what had escaped him until now. His price would be met. It wasn't too high. After he was dead, Gordon would automatically be restored to power. Either way, with or without the papers, he was marked for death before sundown tomorrow.

3.

The driver said, "Coming with me or you going to just stand there mooning, Mister?"

Piers turned, grasping at the straw of friendliness. "Yes." He gave a last backward glance at the doors where she had stood and where she was no longer seen. He climbed back into the cab. Why had she chosen the Metropolitan? To continue the game she'd started, to get hold of herself after the sad sound of memory and love turned to bitterness? To see the pictures?

"Where to?"

Piers considered. "Grand Central."

The cab started. The driver winked again at his mirror. "Better get that lipstick off your face before you take the train, Mister."

"Thanks." He took his handkerchief and rubbed at his mouth.

"If it smells," the driver volunteered, "get you a beer, rub some on your mouth."

"I'll remember that." Piers put the handkerchief away. "Do you know Nick Pulaski?"

The driver considered. "I used to know a Mildred Pulaski once. Worked in a bakery in the Bronx. Is she any relation?"

"I only know Nick," Piers said.

"Might be his sister. They was a big family. Lots of Pulaskis in New York. She was a pretty good-looking girl. Don't know what happened to her. I got changed over to Manhattan. Make more money in Manhattan. The Bronx only tips a dime."

Piers said, "How do you feel about peace?"

"What do you mean?"

"About peace. War and peace."

"There's not going to be any more wars." The driver's face was complacent. "The next big shot that tries to start a war is going to get his head bashed in like a cantaloupe."

"That's the way I feel," Piers said. "But the Germans want the International troops withdrawn. They want to build aeroplanes again. After that guns, and munitions to put in them—"

The driver was vociferously obscene about the Germans.

"I agree," Piers said. No man wanted war. No man had ever wanted war. But the apes smashed stones down on the heads of those things groping through the jungles, watched them turn to rend each other. And the apes scratched their behinds with amused fingers, a substitute for thought.

At 50th the driver said, "I think there's a cab following."

Piers slipped down lower on the upholstery. "Can you see who's in it?"

"No."

She had chosen the Metropolitan. Because there

would be someone to signal there? She knew he had lost his pursuer. It was important to pick Piers up again.

"I want to see who's in it. Any ideas?"

"Are you afraid of getting clipped?"

"No, I'm not." Death was stalking him. And he wasn't afraid. He had a mission to perform; he was certain of carrying it through. He had to carry it through because there was no one else to take over.

"Then I could turn down a side street and when there's no traffic stop. But I don't want no trouble. No shooting."

Piers said, "I don't carry a gun."

"I don't want no corpses in my back seat neither."

"I'll duck." He smiled. "See what you can do"— he re-read the identification tag—"Willie."

"Always a sucker." Willie swung west on 47th. "But I'm curious. And obliging." He reported, crossing Eighth Avenue, "It's following all right. Is it her husband?"

"It isn't a woman," Piers said. "It's peace."

"Are you nuts?" The face was screwed up.

"I'm not nuts. No, Willie. It's peace. The Germans don't want me to show up at the Peace Conclave."

"Well, why didn't you say so?" His ugly face stuck forward. "I got a gun. Got a license for it, too."

Piers said softly, "Don't use it. Unless he attempts something funny." His voice sharpened. "If he does, empty both barrels in the son of a bitch."

"Don't worry."

The cab lost speed. "Don't want them to know

we're tricking," Willie reported. He stopped on the other side of Tenth, in front of a frowsty tenement with kids skating and scrapping on the sidewalk.

Piers shifted to watch the following cab. It had slowed before realizing the maneuver. Now it attempted speed but the passenger was visible as it passed. It was the moon face.

"Recognize him?" Willie asked.

"Yes. German."

"What do we do now?"

"If you can get away from him—" He didn't know where. "Grand Central." It was as safe as any place. The Astor was known and the Plaza. He'd have to find a new hole. He didn't dare use the Lucerne after taking Morgen there. Yet Grand Central wasn't safe; it could hide too many enemies.

"I'll get away. It may cost you."

"I can pay." Piers took two tens, handed them over. "If it's more, all right."

"I wasn't doubting you could pay," Willie said with belligerent ears. "I just didn't know how far you were willing to go."

"All the way."

"That's all I wanted to know." He made a U turn, rolled out of the street the wrong way. Piers didn't follow the labyrinthine trail. He sank back and rested. It must have been Morgen who set them on him again. No one else could.

They were somewhere among warehouses when Willie asked, "You in a bad spot?"

"Desperate."

"If you want a hideout, I could maybe help you."

"I've been trying to think of one. I have no friends."

"Well, it's my brother-in-law. He got in some trouble—he's an Eye-talian—they're hot-blooded. We didn't want Josie to marry him but you know how girls are, with him flashing a big car and she'd been working in a laundry. It wasn't murder, the guy didn't die. Anyhow he's hiding out. We could put you in with him. It's safe."

Piers repeated as if the word were in a foreign tongue. "Safe."

"I can tell you that, it's safe. Me and Josie run in every day or so—bring him food and the papers and a bottle—nobody'd ever find you there."

Piers asked, "I couldn't go in and out?"

"No, sir." The driver shook his head with force. "No, you couldn't do that. You might lead someone to Paulie. But you'd be safe."

"I'm sorry." He was. A place to sleep without fear, beside a criminal. "I'd have to be free to come and go."

Willie's head was doleful. "That's too bad. You'd be safe with Paulie. Grand Central?"

He looked at his watch. After three. He said, "No. If we're clear, take me to Central Park. Uptown, around a Hundred-and-tenth will be all right. Make it the West Side."

Willie cocked an eye at him. "Okay," was all he said.

There was nothing else he could do at the moment unless he chose to walk into the arms of pursuers.

Willie set him down above 110th. The cabbie said, "Wait a minute." He took a dingy card from his pocket and with a wetted stub of pencil printed on it. "If you need help again, you call up this number and ask for Willie. If it gets too hot for you I'll pick you up and take you where Paulie is. It'd be better to stay inside than get bumped off."

Piers said, "Thanks." He put the card in his wallet, watched the reluctant cabman drive away.

He walked up the hill, away from the whir of tires on the drives. There was no sound where he rested but the play of children, a nursemaid humming an old song. Only one day to go; from now until tomorrow's sundown. He must remain free, and alive for that long. He was the only barrier between the success of the apes and peace.

His death had been decreed. Morgen had warned beneath her breath. Because she knew if he came to them tonight, he would die? But she also knew he would not come. Or had her life with Hugo blinded her to the fact that there were men to whom other things were more important than ambition, greed, revenge? On the chance he did come, she would have to report the presumptive sale of his honor to the others. They would believe; they knew man only in their own ape image. Gordon would be told how small he was.

His death was more important to them than the papers now that Gordon was named, now that Anstruther was given up as lost. But for one factor. They couldn't know but that the documents would be automatically passed on to another if he were eliminated.

They didn't know how alone he was, how helpless. Because of that, they would allow him to dangle a little longer in this life before they snuffed him out. They would prefer the treachery of paying a price before the kill. They could afford a few more hours.

There was yet the final move before tomorrow, the retrieving of the memoranda. He would be trailed threefold when he went for them. Unless Willie could help him out. He would recover the papers. True, he would have no voice in the Conclave; Gordon would see to that. Yet if David came tonight, if he could be taken to Fabian, he might yet have a chance. And if David didn't come—voice or not, he would attend the Conclave. The galleries were open to the people. The people could see but the people could not speak. If he could do nothing else, he could give Anstruther's words to the people, there among them. He would make the people speak.

He wasn't beaten. He wouldn't despair. His voice would be the voice of Anstruther and he would be heard. He had only fear to fear. It was fear which had placed him in this far corner of the park alone. Fear or wisdom. Fear that even now, Morgen, in scorn of his warning, would be baiting the trap. Fear that if he didn't attend the proposed meeting, he would be carried there by force.

That was his only fear. Not of death, for he would not die until his time for death was given. But to be made captive, forced to divulge the whereabouts of the papers. He had no fine ideas of his bravery; there had been tortures divined of evil in the Last War

178

which would compel a braver man than he to talk. He must remain free.

Strength was returning in the comparative peace of afternoon in Central Park. If he could but sleep here this night, under the stars. He couldn't. He would have to return to the room which hung above Broadway, return and wait there with his last faint hope of Fabian.

When the sun was low he began to walk, southward, toward the interlocking tower of buildings. He didn't know the miles but it was good to be on his feet, moving. He walked the length of the park and he wasn't tired but he was hungry, a good needful hunger. If he were to be hunted this night, in hiding tomorrow, he would at least have the strength in him of dining well. The vermilion borders of a Longchamps bannered and he went in, but he couldn't taste the food he ordered. He kept watching for someone watching him. He saw no one. It would be ironic if, now that he was prepared for flight, the shadows should be withdrawn. His importance nullified by the solidifying of Gordon's position. No use in fathering that wish.

He wouldn't return to the Astor until an hour when he could slip in unnoticed, unseen. He walked to Fifth, caught a downtown bus. He could ride under the distant stars in the cool of the evening, forget need of plans for a little. He wasn't the only New Yorker with the idea of riding the stars in spring. The top deck was filled. He selected a seat downstairs near the rear door to watch for a descending passenger. He picked up an evening tabloid discarded there, began going over the columns for a possible item on Fabian. His head bent closer to the gossip column.

He read the lines twice and anger was red in him. A pairing of names. Bianca Anstruther and Hugo von Eynar. The sly insinuation that Gordon was definitely relieved over a broken betrothal. The devilish hint that wedding bells might open the Conclave. He read the notice again and he didn't believe it more than gossip but the signature was that of a man presumed by himself and his public to be omniscient. Wedding bells couldn't mean Gordon and Morgen. She was Caesar's wife. It could mean only that Gordon had given the Anstruther child into the unclean hands of Hugo.

He crushed the paper tight in his hand as he pushed the button, flung himself from the bus. He was in the 30's. He strode uptown, not wasting time standing for a cab. He'd attend that meeting tonight. He didn't care if it did mean walking into their trap; he'd been in other of their traps and escaped. This violation was not to be allowed. He'd talked a lot of words about fighting for peace; no longer must they be empty. The disposal of Bianca might have nothing to do with peace but she was all that remained of Anstruther.

This first blow against Hugo would be the preliminary skirmish before the battle for destruction of Germany's wicked plan. But it would count. Hugo should know tonight that all the cards were in Piers' hand, that he intended, despite Gordon, despite Evanhurst, despite Fabian, to play them tomorrow.

At 42nd there was an empty cab waiting and he ordered savagely, "Waldorf Astoria." Only when he was standing at the hotel desk did he know that Hugo wouldn't be lounging here waiting for him. It was too early. The clerk repeated, "Mr. von Eynar is not in."

He set out again, still clutching the paper, caught another cab. "The Plaza." He'd track him through the accustomed haunts. He gave the bellboy a bill and pointed to the Persian Room. "Find out if Hugo von Eynar is in there."

"You want to see him?"

"Yes, I want to see him."

"What name, sir?"

Piers stared at the empty-faced boy. "John Smith." He laughed.

The boy returned without Hugo. Piers went to the desk, asked, "Will you see if Hugo von Eynar is with Lord Evanhurst?"

The clerk stated, "Lord Evanhurst is in Washington."

He turned on his heel. Once more and then he'd have to start guessing. He signaled the first cab. "The Astor." The crawling delay in the side streets, surfeited with theater traffic, was beyond enduring. He paid off and he strode the remaining blocks, cut across Broadway heedless of the pinwheels of traffic. He saw none of the painted couples in the lobby, striding out for the bar. He heard nothing until he was stopped by words, by a big lump of a man in his path.

Cassidy was curious. "Where've you been?"

It was the first realization he had that he was walking back into the surveillance which he had carefully cleared. At the moment it didn't matter. He said, "I'll tell you all about it after I see—"

Cassidy didn't let him pass. "I got something to tell you first."

Piers' eyes saw Cassidy then and he saw the determination in the loose face. His hand tightened over the newspapers. He said, "Please. I just want a few moments with Hugo von Eynar and then I'll—"

"Von Eynar isn't in there."

He hadn't expected this to fail. He let the bitter disappointment ride him.

"None of them are. I got something to tell you. I'll stand you a beer. But I know a better place we can go."

Piers half heard. "Do you know where von Eynar is?"

"Mebbe." The eyes were shrewd. "You going with me?"

"Listen. Please listen. It's important I see Hugo von Eynar—"

"I know." Cassidy's hand was fatherly on his sleeve. "But you better talk to me first."

Piers heard the interlinear message in the words and he saw in the light blue eyes something that was not to be denied. But he couldn't capitulate, the time waste would be unendurable; it was important he face Hugo now while the frenzy burned, before sanity ruled away the words he must fling, turning him craven again. "If you'll tell me where von Eynar is—"

"I'll tell you," Cassidy said. He urged him like a child towards the 44th street entrance. He kept on talking. "I'll tell you anything you want to know. Over a beer it goes better."

Impatient and helpless Piers went along, towards Eighth Avenue, into a small bar that wasn't gilded, one that only its intimates would know. Cassidy nodded to the bartender, "Couple of beers," and he led the way back to the farthest corner.

Piers slumped down. He noticed the paper in his hand and he laid it open on the table, smoothed that column. "Have you seen this?" He pushed it in front of Cassidy.

The detective read slowly. "What about it?"

Each word was venom. "I know Hugo von Eynar. I knew him in the Last War. There's no decency in him. A woman would know that. She's only a little girl. She hasn't any standard of values to go on. I don't intend it shall happen."

Cassidy put the heavy mug to his mouth. "What you planning to do?"

"I don't know." He spoke with cold clarity. "I only know he isn't going to marry Bianca Anstruther. He destroyed her father."

Cassidy said, "After what you said in Devlin's office, I thought you didn't like Germans. I didn't care about seeing you with them last night."

"It turned my stomach," Piers answered. "But I have a job to do." He looked across at the detective. "Maybe in your job you have to be seen with some kind of men you wouldn't spit on."

"Maybe you're right."

Piers put down his mug. "You said you'd tell me where to find von Eynar."

"Yeah. I'm not sure. But Mr. Gordon's having a little dinner party in his suite at the Waldorf. I wouldn't be surprised but you'll find von Eynar there. Mr. Gordon seems kind of friendly to the Germans."

Piers finished his beer. "Thanks. I'll—"

Cassidy's big hand closed over his wrist. Piers looked down at it without comprehension.

"Hold on. Remember I got something to tell you."

"I remember." The impatience to meet with Hugo welled again.

The hand didn't move. "I'm supposed to arrest you tonight."

His wrist bones shrank under the hand. He knew then what Cassidy's ushering of him from the Astor had been like. It wasn't a father guiding a child. It was a detective escorting a prisoner.

"Why?"

Cassidy took away the hand. "That's what I'm going to tell you. You want to buy a beer now?"

"Yes." He had to think; it had come too soon. He'd expected it tomorrow, not today. The waiter in the stained apron brought two more mugs. Piers watched the foam. "So I'm under arrest?"

"Not yet."

Piers' eyes jumped to the steady face.

"I got my orders to bring you in."

"Captain Devlin?"

"The boss."

"What charge?"

"Material witness in the disappearance of Secretary Anstruther."

Piers' eyebrows pulled together. "They can't do that. Secretary Anstruther—" He couldn't tell Cassidy that Secretary Anstruther had met death in Africa and that the jurisdiction of the New York commissioner couldn't extend that far. "Secretary Anstruther—" He took his time. "Do you mean they're saying that Secretary Anstruther isn't going to return?"

"They're saying he's missing. The radio and newspapers. Winchell went on the air special tonight saying Anstruther's missing and that every mother's son in New York better turn up at the Conclave tomorrow to stand up for peace. He named you as the guy that knows too much. The government isn't talking but they had to do something. My boss thinks if you're locked up, you can be made to give up those papers you have."

Piers said then, "How does the New York police figure in this?"

"Samuel Anstruther was a New York citizen."

"I see." He drank thoughtfully. "Who directed the Commissioner?" He eyed the man. "You see I happen to know that all news of the Secretary was to be suppressed until after the Conclave opens. I heard that from the President himself."

Cassidy said, "It's a request from the President himself."

Behind that a request from Gordon. It could have come from no one else. The President wouldn't ask that Piers Hunt be locked up for investigation concerning Anstruther. The President didn't know that Piers Hunt counted, scarcely knew he existed. The order would come, possibly signed but unread, at Gordon's prod.

That was Gordon's answer to his defiance. Not to fire him from the Commission. That would cause too much speculation at this time; it would hurtle the fact of a missing Secretary into the faces of the representatives. Furthermore Gordon possibly held a residue of fear that Anstruther might return, that he would have to answer to Anstruther. He shook his head. The clever Gordon, the superb Gordon, the damnable Gordon. Ridding himself of the threat of Piers so simply, with legal astuteness, the safety of it. He damned Gordon from silent white lips. Then he saw Cassidy. "Why have you told me this?"

The detective scrubbed his cheek as if he needed thought for an answer. "I'll tell you. Maybe it's like this. Devlin and me were in secret service in the Last War. We saw a lot of funny things. Folks that were on our side being made to look like they weren't. And folks against us purring up to the right parties and fooling those parties. We kind of talked it over, Devlin and me, and we believe you meant what you said yesterday. We think you're for peace. Maybe someone's trying to make it look like you aren't but we kind of believe you meant what you said." His eyes hardened now. "If we're wrong, well, I'll pick you up easy. I've never lost a man I've been after."

Piers didn't smile. "Then I'm not under arrest."

"You broke away from me when we got to Broadway. Better keep out of my sight though. When I see you again I'll have to run you in. It'll go worse for you then. But you can have the chance if you want it."

"I want it." He added, "You'll get hell for this, Cassidy."

Cassidy looked at him as if he were very young. "I've been in the game a long time, boy. I've watched them come and go. I'm not worried about this boss. All I'm worried about is war. I've been through two already."

Piers said, "Gordon isn't going to like it."

Cassidy wiped the heel of his hand across his mouth. "Neither is that German woman who was with him down to the Commissioner's office."

Piers' eyes shuttered.

"She says you were trying to sell her the Anstruther papers."

"That was how they got the Presidential request." He spoke to himself. He, the idiot child, believing Morgen's betrayal would be predictable. It had never been.

"I don't like Germans," Cassidy said. "Three of my boys came back from the Last War; three didn't. I don't like Germans mixing in our business."

Piers pushed back his chair, holding the newspaper. "Thanks." He put out his hand to clasp Cassidy's. "You haven't bet the wrong horse. Maybe it'll look like it before tomorrow, but you haven't."

"I'm a poor loser," Cassidy said. "I don't bet only on sure things."

"How long a start are you giving me?"

Cassidy shook his head. "I'll be right here with Mike and my beer until bedtime. Tomorrow . . ."

VII

Tomorrow he'd be safe or he'd be dead. There was a cab up the block near 44th street. Piers wasn't reckless now; he avoided it, plunging around the corner to 45th, walking quickly towards the lights. The uncle might yet be following although presumedly he'd be called off with Piers' fate taken in hand by the New York police. Safe behind bars.

On Broadway he picked up a cruiser and rode back to the Waldorf. Despite the dangers he had to finish this. After, he'd hide out until tomorrow.

He didn't know the suite number; he asked at the desk. "De Witt Gordon."

The clerk knew the important Gordon of the Peace Commission. He looked quickly at Piers but tonight Piers wasn't rag and bobtail. The man was courteous. "Your name, please?"

Piers said without hesitation, "Watkins. From Washington."

He waited until the call was completed. "Go right up, Mr. Watkins. Suite C. The fourteenth floor."

The elevator was crowded. Gordon wouldn't be suspicious, not with Evanhurst in Washington, not with secret business that must be completed before the opening tomorrow. Hugo might not be here. Gordon might call the police; Schern or Brecklein might attack. Piers had no weapon; he wished he had but he hadn't owned one since the declaration of peace. What he did have was stronger than weapons; his knowledge against their desire for knowledge. They wanted it yet; orders to bring him in wouldn't have been given otherwise. A bullet in the dark would have been a quicker solution.

He knocked on the suite door. Gordon himself opened it. He frowned, "I didn't expect you."

Piers pushed in. "I'm Watkins."

They were there, still at the betrothal table. And they were motionless while he looked them over one by one. Bianca, the happiness fading from her young face under his study; Hugo, accentuating his malicious arrogance with lifted eyeglass; Morgen, more beautiful than the red roses on her breast, more treacherous than the scent of bitter almonds. The older men must have gone with Evanhurst to Washington. They would not be needed here; the book on Piers was closed with Gordon's orders given.

"Close the door," Piers told Gordon.

Disturbed, he did as he was bid. "I don't understand."

"You will." He gestured Gordon back to the others. "I'm before time again, Morgen," he said. He took the newspaper from his pocket. "But I thought I'd best have a private talk with Hugo before business. Ever since I read this. I've escaped from Cassidy just now for one reason, to ask if this is true."

Hugo took Bianca's hand. "Certainly it's true. Aren't you going to congratulate me?"

"No, I'm not."

Hugo's smile curled around the young girl.

"I have no intention of allowing you to get away with it."

Gordon's shoulders broadened. "I'm afraid I must ask you to leave, Piers."

"You sit down." He didn't raise his voice; he was careful not to raise his voice. The sound might stir physical violence. It was ugly enough without that. "You don't know any more than Bianca does what this is all about. You poor insular fool."

Hugo was on his feet now and the glass dropped from his eye. "What are you attempting to say?"

"I'm saying it. You aren't going to sacrifice Secretary Anstruther's daughter for the Fatherland. If she and Gordon weren't a couple of children they'd see through it but they haven't had enough experience to know what you are."

"And what is that?" The ice over his words was brittle.

Piers said, "I don't believe you wish me to answer that . . . here." He looked from Hugo to Morgen and again at Hugo.

Bianca rushed beside Hugo now, her hand under his arm. She said, "I don't know what kind of madman you are bursting in here, evidently with the intention of interfering with Hugo's and my plans. Your impudence is only exceeded by your stupidity."

He asked brutally, "Do you know what von Eynar wants with you?"

190

Her lips spattered scorn.

"Don't get the idea it's because you're round and young and warm that he'll marry you. I won't say that doesn't count with Hugo but that isn't enough. He's had better than you." The words were thorns in his mouth.

A gust of anger bruised her. "How dare you say such things?" She turned to Gordon frantically, "Witt, can't you do something?"

Piers blocked both the telephone table and the door. "He can't. Once he was strong enough but not now." His hands closed over the back of a chair and he set it purposefully in front of him. "Not since he became Hugo's pimp."

The rage leapt in Gordon, and Piers lifted the chair slightly.

Bianca was white as pearl. "Hugo is my fiancé."

"Yesterday it was Witt. Tomorrow?"

"We are to be married tomorrow." She thrust it at him.

Piers' mouth twisted at Hugo. "No time to waste, is there? The Secretary just might return before the Conclave. He couldn't very well move against his daughter's husband." He turned on the girl. "Couldn't you see that? Don't you know you're just a small pawn in Germany's game?"

She moved closer to Hugo. He didn't sense her. He was watching Piers, waiting.

Morgen spoke gently, almost with casualness. "More melodrama, Piers?"

He moved his eyes on her. She hadn't stirred from the chair. She alone here didn't fear or hate him because she alone didn't care. He looked at her and the want of her as always rose like nostalgia for a beloved city, and the hate of her twisted in his heart. He asked, "Have you an answer for me yet, Morgen?" He put his eyes hard on Gordon as if Gordon didn't know. "I opened the bidding today on the Anstruther papers."

Bianca's cry was strangled.

Gordon said, "You can't do that, Piers. They belong to me now."

"I can do it," Piers said. "Because you can't get at them without playing dice with me. You didn't think of that. You double-crossed me. Bound me to secrecy and then ran fast to the chief. You knew how to step into Anstruther's shoes, didn't you? You didn't realize that you wouldn't know how to fill them. If you were that big, you wouldn't have to hold the tin cup for the von Eynars. You wouldn't need to throw Bianca to the beasts."

Morgen said, "Don't be absurd, Piers." She was untouched. "Because Bianca and Witt made a normal mistake—"

"It's Gordon who made the mistake, dear. He thought you could help him. He believed you when you told him that once he held the nominal power of the Secretary, he could discount me. I could be forced to turn over to him my information. By the way, Gordon, has Nickerson cabled you that the office was broken into and all papers pertaining to my work stolen? Sad. More so because there was nothing in the files concerning our present problems. You see, I've worked before against Schern. I knew the need of

192

precaution." He smiled. "Won't you sit down, Bianca? You look so tired standing there. You too, Hugo. Gordon? This will take a little time."

No one moved.

He shrugged. "Well, Morgen, how much was I bid for Secretary Anstruther's papers? I have them, you know. You've known that all along, haven't you? Ever since the Arab who switched the dispatch cases reported to you. I'm afraid I broke his wrist. But so stupid for him to tell me it wasn't Anstruther's case when I could see the initials—three faded gold initials, Ulysses Samuel Anstruther. You know for what that stands? The next man you hire should be warned to respect those initials."

Bianca breathed, "You killed my father."

He paid no attention to her incoherency. Her reason had been corrupted by von Eynar. "Was my price met, Morgen? Or did they attempt to cut it. A directorship in German Airways, Inc.? I'm certain Brecklein wouldn't hesitate to offer that. Particularly since an accident so easily can occur in the line of duty. A million gold? Schern would think of that; he has always believed money could buy any man. After the man is corrupted, it is simple enough to get back the gold. What did Hugo offer? But of course. He has only one thing of value to offer—you."

"You are insufferable," Hugo said.

"Did you agree to offer Morgen? I'll admit that is beyond value. And tempting. Easy enough to get her back, too. You need only to kill me and beckon."

Gordon's face was mottled.

"The trouble is I don't want any substitutes. Not

even you, Morgen." Only with his blood and nerves and sinews. "Would you like to hear what it is I want, Gordon?"

"I don't know why we put up with this," Hugo said.

Piers knew then that he was armed. The flex of his right hand, the threat on his mouth. Gordon wasn't. But Gordon was taunted beyond reason. His speech was thick. "I don't care what you want."

Morgen commanded, "Let him speak." The men were held in check. "Tell them what it is you asked."

He smiled at her. "It isn't much, is it, my dear?" He moved his eyes to Gordon. "I want Gordon's head. I want to ruin Gordon."

Bianca cried out, "That's why you killed my father! Because you wanted to be Secretary."

He said gently, "But I didn't kill him, Bianca. The man who killed him was a friend of Hugo's. They were in the Luftwaffe together."

Bianca cried, "Stop him, Hugo."

Hugo spoke with impatience. "Be quiet, Bibi. What do his lies matter? I haven't seen Gundar in twelve years."

"You understand? Hugo names him, not I. Your father was shot in the back, Bianca, by Hugo's friend." He watched the horror eating her away. He said with tight throat, "I didn't want you to know, not this way. But it's the least I can do for a man I loved. Protect the thing he loved best. I wouldn't want to see you after a year with Hugo."

Bianca faded into the chair. She put her head on

her arms. No one paid any attention to her. Morgen was on her feet now. The men started forward.

Piers said sharply, "Don't come any nearer. You don't want to harm me, not until you have the papers. Even if I am gone, they still can speak."

Morgen demanded, "What happened to the Secretary? You know?"

"That's the one thing has kept you from killing me, isn't it? Your fear that the Secretary might return. Because Gundar Abersohn never came back with his report. He couldn't come back, you see. He's dead too. It's strange you didn't find the graves."

Hugo said, "There were no graves. Only the wreckage of a plane. But no humans had perished in the fire."

He didn't understand. The jackals . . . His jaw trembled. "I didn't come to remember what is past. I came to see if my price is to be met. Where is Schern? We must finish this now. Cassidy might catch up with me before tomorrow."

Morgen and Hugo moved together. He knew what their eyes said. He shook his head. "No, it isn't safe to eliminate me even now, now that you know Anstruther is dead. Because I've another card up my sleeve. I have your letters, Hugo. The ones concerning the border incidents."

He watched the import of it strike them.

"It wouldn't be wise to eliminate me until you have them, would it? It would be embarrassing for your cause if they turned up tomorrow over my dead body." He smiled. "I'll be more generous than you would be. I'll give up the Anstruther memoranda and the letters in exchange for Gordon's head."

Gordon's head was moving from side to side as if the thread-hung Damoclean sword glittered above it.

Hugo said, "We must talk with Schern. He's in Washington."

"There isn't much time," Piers reminded him. "Only tonight. Tomorrow—if I read in the papers tomorrow that by Presidential order I am to preside at the Conclave until Secretary Anstruther arrives, you will receive both sets of papers."

"Do you think we'd trust you?" Morgen stood motionless.

"No more than I trust you. I won't give you my hand on the bargain. I prefer you where you are. But when I read that notice, I will allow Morgen to carry to you the papers. Come, Morgen."

Her eyes widened.

"You didn't think I'd leave without a hostage? Morgen goes with me."

Gordon broke out of numbness. "No!"

"If there's any difficulty," Piers continued easily, "she will die. Neither of you gentlemen wishes harm to come to Morgen. That is why I take her. You didn't know, Gordon, that she isn't Hugo's sister? Once she was his wife. Until he learned she was of more value not. Naturally you haven't been told. I doubt even that Schern knows. I learned by accident —years ago." His eyes warned. "I would advise you to allow us to leave in peace. Peace." The laughter died in his mouth. "Do you remember when we believed that we could hold the world in peace? Tomorrow by high noon I must know. Morgen—"

She had started to an inner door. "My wrap—"

"No. I don't trust you out of sight, my darling. The night will keep you warm."

"Don't go with him, Morn." Gordon tried to catch her arm. "There's no reason for it. He can't hurt me. We can handle him. We have all the powers of my government behind me."

"You don't have the papers," Piers said softly. "You don't have the word that will keep Germany under protectorate for fifty years."

"It isn't important." Gordon held her. "He can't do anything. He isn't Anstruther."

"You don't have the letters that will put Hugo in the International Court."

Hugo spoke coldly, "Go, Morgen."

Gordon said, "You mustn't!" while she moved, her gallant head high, with her mouth smiling, her eyes cloaked in silence. She went to Piers and she said, "I am ready."

He opened the door, still watching the others. He smiled. "Don't send after me. I'd hate any harm to come to Morgen. I, too, have loved her."

2.

Morgen asked, "Where are we going?" The wind blew in her hair and across her uncovered shoulders.

"I don't know." Only now when they were on the street, walking without direction, did he know fear again. It had been a foolhardy adventure, no more, for of what use was a deed for a man who was dead, who could never know? The girl wasn't worth it. "I don't know where to go."

"You're not safe on the street," she said.

"I'm not safe anywhere. They're after me, all of them." He had no will to fight at the moment. He was exhausted in spirit and in will. The semi-darkness of Madison was retreat, and the silence of Morgen. But behind them in the darkness the hunters padded, a moon-faced German, a dark bushman. Tonight Cassidy wasn't standing between him and death.

"Ernst won't be back from Washington until to-morrow. We can double back. My rooms will be safe."

His savage laughter was his answer. And they walked on.

She asked, "What was the reason for all that mumbo jumbo at Witt's?" Scorn was staccato. "You don't care about that girl."

"No, I don't care about that girl."

"Why walk into danger? Did you believe I'd actually arrange your fantastic meeting?"

"Have I changed that much?"

She searched his face. "No. You've changed very little. That's why I don't understand how it is you came tonight."

"You sold me out to Witt."

"No."

"To the Commissioner. Why?"

She said, "To get the papers. You knew I would."

"Did you think Gordon would turn them over to you?"

Her voice was sweet as bells. "He had no choice."

He caught her shoulders. "What do you mean?"

"Don't you know what I mean? That is his part of the bargain." Her eyes dared his. He knew what she could mean, Gordon a deliberate traitor, not an addled fool. He also knew her dishonesty. He walked on again.

"I offered you the papers. For a right price. You didn't need to sell me out."

She said, "You had no intention ever of giving up the papers to us."

He said nothing.

"Did you?"

"Not ever," he told her flatly.

"Why did you pretend? Did you think I would believe you?"

This was the last night. There were but two alternatives for tomorrow, success or failure, peace or war. It didn't matter what he told her now. It wouldn't change tomorrow. "I wanted to get at Gordon. There was only one way, through you. The man is armored; he has always been. I never knew there was a weak link until I saw him look at you, that night in my room. I didn't want a strong Gordon tomorrow. I must be present at the Conclave; I must speak."

But it had been a mistake to make the final gesture, to take her away from them. He wished to God he hadn't. It had strengthened them, weakened himself. Fear alone had prompted it, fear that without her he would not leave that room alive. He had believed he could return to his room safely with her as hostage but he had been thinking against time and against force at that moment.

199

Now his brain had clarified. David must come tonight in answer to his personal; there was only tonight. She couldn't be in on the meeting with David. Only one thing was important for him tonight, to wait for David, try to get to Fabian. He must be rid of her.

She was silent, only their steps were heard, drum beats, heart beats on the night. And she said suddenly, "I don't care what they decide. I'll give you Gordon."

He waited, "What price now?"

"Those letters Hugo wrote."

He saw then he couldn't be rid of her easily; she would remain with him until she had those letters. She knew what was in them. Unless he could escape her. And with all of his knowledge and his hatred, the sickness of jealousy pitted him. He taunted, "Not the Anstruther papers?"

"I don't care about them now."

When it came to the final reckoning Hugo alone mattered to her. The schemes of Schern and Brecklein, the Fatherland, all lost importance when Hugo's self was threatened. Or perhaps it was that she knew that Piers wasn't going to be allowed to produce the Anstruther memoranda at the conference. She had been wrong once before. It might be that knowledge which made her less sure of the Hugo letters also being obliviated. She couldn't take the chance because if they were given, they were a death warrant for her lover. And although it started again the internal bleeding, it was because of this quality, this humanness, that he had loved her. Because she too could love, even if it were not he who was loved.

But his mouth was cruel. "And Gordon goes the way of all the others. The Baal Hugo hungers again."

She kept her face ahead. "Will you trade?"

"Give him to me."

"First those letters."

Without halting, he put his hand against the coolness of her hair, turned her head. "Even now, when it is needful you trust, you don't trust me."

"No."

They moved on. He was suddenly harsh. "You know the contents of those letters. You know they would convict Hugo of instigating war. With the implication of connivance in the Secretary's death."

She said, "Hugo had nothing to do with the death."

"It was you?"

"No." This time her steps halted. "Give me the letters. I'll give you the plot against Anstruther."

"Could you?" He laughed down into her face. "Not good enough, my darling. It's too late. I have myself to think of. I must have Gordon. We'll wait for tomorrow."

The shadow of a tree fell across her eyes. One tree by an old brick wall.

He laughed again. "You think I'll be dead tomorrow."

She stood there looking up at him.

"Would you grieve, Morgen?" He shook his head. "I should grieve if you were to die. You are too beautiful to die." He put his hands on her face, pushing away her hair. "Strange that evil can be so beautiful."

She whispered, "I think you're mad."

"No. I'm terribly sane. Only a man as sane as I knows that no price is too great to pay for peace. No one's death is important for peace. Not yours, not Anstruther's. Not even Hugo's. Or mine."

Her voice was still mute. "Did you take me away to kill me?"

"No, dearest. Your death wouldn't help peace. If it would, I shouldn't hesitate. But I must warn you, too many have died through me—without my wish. It isn't wise that you should be with me tonight." His eyes held hers. "What is your part to be in the New Germany?"

"I have no part."

"Only to be behind Hugo. And his part?"

She closed her eyes. The lashes were dark on her shadowed cheeks.

"You might as well tell me." He taunted, "After all I won't be here to see it. Will I?"

She opened her eyes then. They were proud. "Hugo is the new leader. The Führer whom every man will follow. No maniacal Austrian this time. Germany triumphant in the new Siegfried." There was fanatical pride shining out of her face.

He stepped away from her. The enormity of their madness staggered him. The pattern had been used before with such near perfection; it could be consummated. The Germans had hunger for a leader. Hitler had failed them. Hugo wouldn't.

He said, "No." The decision of an avenging god must have been in him. She made a sound of fear.

"Will you give me Witt Gordon's head now, Morgen? Not for any scraps of paper. Because with it I can preserve peace. And in preserving peace I preserve Hugo. If tomorrow is the end of peace, he must die."

Courage was flowing into her. "First the letters."

"They aren't in my pockets." He walked on and she followed. "I carry danger with me but not the dangerous."

She said, "I'm tired. If you won't come to my room, why don't we go to yours?"

"Aren't you being obvious, Morgen? My room has been searched, doubly searched."

"Before you took the letters."

"How do you know?"

"Because I know you didn't have them until Wednesday night, the night you entered the Peace office."

"Under the nose of Uncle Johann Schmidt," he grimaced. "But you didn't know anything important was missing. No, darling, we won't go to my rooms. Too many outstretched arms are awaiting me there."

"There are ways to enter without anyone seeing."

"You know that?" he smiled.

"There are certain to be ways. You want Gordon." She caught his arm. "I can't walk all night. You'll have to decide something."

His eyes dropped to her slippers, twists of colored silk coiled on stilted golden heels. He pointed to the flickering sign a block away. "We'll have a drink and decide." He took her arm and pushed her forward.

The place was down at the heels and the eyes of the

too few customers were resentful of her exquisiteness. Piers didn't care. He propelled her to the back of the long bar. "Champagne or absinthe, beloved?"

She looked across at the bartender. Piers was afraid then she meant to speak, to give him over. He had forgotten that he was wanted. It had been a mistake to allow her to divert him.

But she didn't betray him. She said, "I'll take what you wish, Piers."

He ordered, "Two brandies." The liquor burned him. He looked at Morgen, the way her hair lay against her cheek, the way red roses scented her breast. He didn't want a hostage. He wanted only somewhere to lay his head. He put his hand against her arm. "You'd best go back to Hugo."

"No," she said.

He struck, "He doesn't want you empty-handed."

Her face held the beauty of a beloved. "He wants me any way I come to him."

The truth seared him and he said angrily to the bartender, "Another brandy." He swallowed it in one draught.

She said, "Have you decided where we go?"

It came to him then, that simply. How to hold the hostage and to escape her. His eyes narrowed. "He wants you but you won't go empty-handed, is that it?"

She was silent.

He smiled at her. "If you'll take me to Fabian, I'll give you the letters."

Her mouth was small with anger. "I don't know where he is. No one knows. Not even Gordon."

"I'd be safe there. No one knows."

She put down her glass. "We can't continue like this. I'll go wherever you say."

He lifted her fingers, turned her hand and touched the palm. "Devotion. Moving, isn't it?"

She said, "Call a cab, Piers. We can't stay here."

He smiled at her. "Yes." She had made the suggestion. Call a cab. Call Willie. He took the card from his pocket. "I'll do that, dear one. I even know where we'll be safe. With a murderer. But you won't mind that." Willie could take care of her. Piers would leave her safe with Willie. He wouldn't be stricken until they had Morgen again.

He walked to the phone booth at the front of the room. He didn't touch the handle of the door. He had glimpsed outside the pane the round shadowy face of the German hireling. Anger shot into him; now that he had made his plans he wouldn't have them thwarted by the follower. He strode to the door. He heard Morgen calling after him, "Piers—wait—"

He pushed outside. The man was starting fast across the street. Piers ran, he caught the coatsleeve, swung the dumpy figure about. The moon face stammered with sudden fright. Piers said, "Sorry. I don't want you tonight." He drew back his fist and he thudded it against the jaw. The man fell heavily. His head broke against the curb.

"Piers!" She screamed it now.

He said bitterly, "I suppose he has a weak heart." The man lay without motion.

"Piers!"

From the bar doorway, the curious were emerging. He had to let her go, to take his chances alone. There was nothing else to do. If the police took him, he would never see Fabian or peace. He turned her to him. "I can't carry you further. Not now. Don't try to follow me. Good-by, Morgen." He kissed her and then he ran crazily into the dark side street with her screaming and the sudden shouts of the bystanders after him.

He ran faster than they could run. He couldn't have retraced his path, ducking, twisting, lurking, cutting back. He didn't know the block where he found a subway kiosk; it was somewhere on Lexington. He felt the breath of pursuit as he clattered down the steps, fumbled for a nickel, and pushed past the turnstile just in time to catch the train roaring in. But they weren't behind him; the stairs and platform were empty when the train jerked out again.

When the Sixties appeared he knew it was a downtown subway. His breath began to modulate and he straightened his tie and coatsleeve. He'd lost his hat when he ran. It didn't matter. She'd give his name to the police when they came but they already had the name. He wondered if the uncle of Johann Schmidt actually had a weak heart. The man had lain so still. He wondered if he had held the power of death again in his hand.

He left the train at Grand Central and shuttled to Times Square. When he emerged to the street, Broadway was as untouched, as beautiful and garish and heartless as always. She didn't know the battle being waged on her doorstep against one of her children; if she knew she wouldn't care. She had too many chil-

dren to care about one. She would know nothing until the bombs fell again.

He walked on the opposite side from the Astor. He
lifted his eyes to the fifth floor window, that center
window. He thought there was a shadow but he didn't
know. He couldn't enter through the lobby; Cassidy
had warned him not to be seen again tonight. It
wouldn't be Cassidy alone after him now; the call
would have gone out to the department from Gordon
as soon as he left the Waldorf. They weren't afraid of
him. Not now with Anstruther known dead.

Morgen knew a way in not through the lobby. So
did he, if no guards were on the door. Now that he
had run from Morgen the want of her was in him
again. He could have had her with him this night, for
comfort against the cold of tomorrow. Despair was
fogging him anew. There was no way that his voice
could be heard tomorrow, not without Fabian. Fabian
must speak for him. David would come. The Africans
too knew it was the last night; they must have seen his
message by now.

He circled to the service entrance and he hesitated.
But he couldn't hesitate; he must go on. There was
no one seeming to watch it. He went inside; he wasn't
challenged. He climbed the stairs until the count
said the fifth floor. He had miscalculated. He descended one flight, went still unchallenged to his own
door. He put in the key and opened it. Only when he
stood in the open doorway did it occur to him that he
might have been shot down as he entered, that the
enemy could have been waiting here. It was then he

saw in the half-darkness the figure against the far wall.

"David." Unbelieving, he uttered his relief.

"Come in quietly and close the door." Hugo's voice was stone. "I am waiting. You are covered by my gun."

Piers closed the door and he stood there while the lights lifted, bright and red and blue. He saw the blunt barrel of the automatic, the protuberance of a silencer within it. He didn't move. "Why are you here?"

"Those letters. You will give them to me."

He took his time. "You offer me my life in exchange?"

"I offer you nothing. I have come for those letters."

Piers asked mildly, "If these were so important, why were they kept in open files?"

Hugo said, "They were harmless unless you should read them. You who know too much."

"Too much to live?"

"Exactly."

Piers took a breath. "I don't intend to die."

Hugo's mouth was scornful.

"I don't think I will die until you know what I have done with Morgen."

The immobility was shaken. "Morgen—" He brazened. "She led you here and she escaped. You are bluffing."

That had been the plan, not for her to get the letters from him but to lead him to Hugo. She knew where Hugo would wait. And if she couldn't lead Piers there—but she knew and Hugo knew he would return here tonight. They had seen and understood the message to David. They would even know David; with them nothing was left to chance.

Piers shrugged. "Then kill me. You aren't going to get the letters yet."

Hugo's voice chunked the words. "Where is Morgen?"

"She is safe." He asked lightly, "How did you get into this room?"

"Where is Morgen?"

"You don't believe that she is safe for the present? Why don't you search for her? Or is that beneath the dignity of the new Führer?"

Hugo hardened. "You have found that out."

"Morgen told me. We are old friends, you remember? What did you and Bianca decide?"

Hugo asked, "Why did Morgen tell you?"

His voice was soft. "I persuaded her, shall we say?"

The lights showed the labor of Hugo's mind. "If you have injured her—"

"Injured Morgen? I who saved her from the International Judgment?"

He said harshly, "That you might deal in your own fashion."

"Vengeance is the Lord's, Hugo. If I had wanted it, could I not have carried it out long ago?"

"Not as now. Now when we are ready for fulfillment. Morgen has worked for this—that I may ascend my rightful place."

"Don't say too much," Piers warned.

"Why not? You won't repeat this. Even if you should, you have been discredited. The United States

Government is seeking you. The man who killed Anstruther, stole his papers for his own use."

Piers was fired with rage. He didn't care about the gun; he was a man of peace but he would have killed Hugo at this moment with his bare hands had Hugo been Gordon. His fists tightened but he spoke quietly. "You're saying a lot of words, Hugo. We call it whistling in the dark." Hugo wasn't going to kill him. He was to live to settle with Gordon. "You don't have the Anstruther papers. You don't have the African letters." His mouth twisted. "You don't have Morgen."

Hugo was gusseted with doubt. Had he, Piers, been armed, he could have winged him then. The man was off guard. Piers pressed on. "You are easily taken in, you new Germans. Just as were the old. Do you remember the Russian campaign? You've believed that Gordon was discrediting me. You haven't looked deeper. You haven't considered that we too could play a game to discredit you."

Hugo's smile was confident. "Gordon is our man, Piers. We didn't have to convince him; he came to us three years ago in Rio. He planned Anstruther's death, not us."

Piers knew Hugo lied. He'd listened to German lies so often. Gordon was their man, yes, but out of passion and ignorance. Piers' lip curled, "You put guilt on him for the plan, on me for the fulfillment?" He shook his head. His suggestion was mendacious as Hugo's own. "I know Schern's treacherous touch too well for that, Hugo. You think the police are after me because Gordon told you that? It has never occurred to you that they were put on me to protect me? That this room is under constant surveillance? That Cassidy will be up here soon to make his regular check? Then what will you do, Hugo? If something has happened to me, you will face the law."

Doubt riddled Hugo. It wouldn't have shaken Schern but Hugo wasn't a diplomat, he was a decoration. He spoke with anger out of his unsureness. "I don't want any more words. I want those letters."

"After you have them, you will kill me?"

The mask of the beast was over his face. "Turn out your pockets."

"They aren't on me."

"Turn them out."

"You're not afraid I'll pull a gun?"

Hugo said, "We know you do not carry a gun." There was no doubt that the dossier was definite.

Piers shrugged. He emptied his pockets on the bedspread. He did it slowly, spreading out the scant display, opening the billfold to show its innocence. He even laid the key-ring there—with such a number of keys Hugo could not recognize an important one. "Nothing, you see."

Hugo walked to them, the gun still pointed. He touched them apart. "Where are the letters?"

Piers was silent.

Hugo lifted the gun and he struck Piers across the mouth with it. Piers tasted blood and helpless fury.

Hugo repeated without inflection, "Where are they?"

He said bitterly, "Where you will never lay hands on them." He added, "No matter what you do."

Hugo's mouth smiled but his eyes were inhuman. He said, "You've had your chance. Morgen didn't want you to die. Not for any reason you think. Because she thought I might be involved. But no one saw me enter this room. I know because I was covered when I came in. No one will know who killed you."

For the first time the reality smote Piers; he was to die. He was to stand here and die. And with him would die the hope for peace.

"I have a silencer. I know you are not protected by the police; I know Gordon better than you. If you did pass the letters to someone else, I'll let Schern take care of that. Without your word to corroborate them, they won't be of much use. I don't believe they'll be any danger with you out of the way."

Piers drew forth again the weapon he'd counted on, his last chance. "You may kill me, yes, and what about Morgen?"

Again there was the faintest hesitation. And in the silence from his stand near the door, Piers heard the elevator doors open, heard the footsteps approaching his room. David now, too late. And quickly he knew he was wrong; David did not walk with sound. It was the police. He had spoken truth without knowing, the police would keep checking on his room. He couldn't escape the law now; he could escape death. He smiled.

Hugo didn't understand the smile. He raged, "You're lying about Morgen, too. You wouldn't have hurt Morgen, she means too much for you."

"One thing I wasn't lying about," Piers said. "The police detective is coming to this door right now."

Hugo backed into deeper shadow.

"You can't kill me, not and get away with it. It's too late now, Hugo. He'll take me. The government will have the letters before tomorrow."

Hugo's mouth moved. "Stand away from that door. Let him come in."

He realized with sudden horror what Hugo meant to do. Only the beast was there; another killing meant nothing. And as he realized he suddenly recognized the steps. They were not those of a man. The rap sounded.

"Stand away. And say nothing."

His throat was dry. "You can't do it. You won't get away with it. It's murder."

"Quiet."

"The law will take you." The sweat stood on his temples, in his eyes. "You can't escape no matter what you do. You can't lie to Cassidy—he doesn't like Germans." He was pushing, pushing the man to the brink of fear, of self-control. His teeth cut into his broken mouth. "I'll live and I'll have the letters. You've lost. Put away the gun."

Hugo's word was a snarl. "Quiet."

He heard the pass key in the lock, the knob turning. The lights from Broadway faded. That alone he couldn't plan. As the door swung open in the darkness, Hugo fired the silenced shot. She walked into it, kept walking.

Hugo's face was raw. "Morgen!" The lights came up. He cried it, "Morgen!"

Her mouth opened but only blood came out. She crumpled and she lay there, moving, but without movement. Piers closed the door. He saw the gun

213

where it had fallen from Hugo's hand but he didn't move. Hugo stumbled forward, knelt to her.

Piers' throat closed. "Don't touch her!"

Hugo didn't hear. Piers circled to the gleam on the rug. He picked it up and pointed it at the man. There was agony beneath the numbness. He repeated, *"Don't touch her!"*

Hugo raised his head. His empty eyes saw Piers. "You killed her." His voice was livid as a wound. "You killed her!" He came to his feet. "You knew she was there."

Piers said, "It was her life or mine. Mine was more important." The smile was terrible on his face. "She died for you. And you will die for her, for murdering her."

Hugo's voice was without feeling. "I hate you. I've hated you since the days of Berlin. You and your sanctimony. You and your arrogant righteousness, while you were signaling the bombs to destroy my country. I wanted to kill you the first night I met you. Morgen wouldn't let me. She liked your pretty face."

"She loved me," Piers said. He was trying to understand. "It wasn't something she could explain. But she loved me. The way she might have loved the good if she'd ever had a chance to know it."

Hugo moved as in a dream. "I'm going to kill you."

Piers said quietly, "I have your gun."

"You killed Morgen. I'll kill you." He was whispering it, like one mad, and he kept moving.

Piers held the gun steady and then willfully he thrust it away. He didn't want Hugo to die. He wanted him to be destroyed and to live, to live as he,

214

Piers, would live and grieve. He needed no arms with which to battle Hugo; it must be tooth and claw alone.

As for himself, he knew now he was not to die. He had the gift of death for others, not for himself. The gift he had borne to Anstruther, to a nameless man on Broadway, in full knowledge to Morgen. The hate in him matched the hate in Hugo as they met. The lights faded, the lights glittered, with the unendurable ceaseless rhythm of a heart, of the cosmos. She lay white and silent, not seeing the beasts that tore at each other, because she was dead. This was jungle, only jungle ways were valid.

There was fresh blood in Piers' mouth, the blood of his enemy wetted his thumbs. They fell, beating, scraping at each other. And in the heat Piers saw her face, the stillness of it, the desolation on her mouth, the stain spreading below the roses on her breast. All of his judgment on the man who had forced him to destroy her went into that last blow. Hugo was still.

Piers' breath jerked. The faint residue of man-spirit in him alone kept him from killing the beaten man where he lay. He rose unsteadily. He rasped, "Get up."

Hugo lay quiet. Another weak heart? He stirred the body with his toe. "Get up. Finish it."

Hugo didn't move. Piers took out his handkerchief, wiped at the blood on his face. He didn't see the quick grasping movement. He heard the report of the silenced gun and the sting in his shoulder. He fell on Hugo before he could fire again and he broke the gun out of the man's hand. He didn't use it. His fists beat the final blows.

Hugo twitched and was still. This time he wouldn't move. Piers swayed to his feet again. He looked at the gun in his hand. Mechanically he broke it, removed the shells. He didn't want to be shot in the back. He didn't trust Hugo von Eynar even when he lay unconscious. Piers dropped the empty gun beside Hugo's hand. His own prints covered it, his and Hugo's. It didn't matter now. If Germany won tomorrow, nothing mattered. If they lost, his truth of tonight would be accepted. He wiped his mouth again and he walked to the door.

He didn't look at Morgen.

3.

He walked without seeing to the service stairway and he started down. Slowly, as a man dreaming, one step, two, and then he heard and he was frozen there listening. Footsteps ascending, the heavy footsteps of heavy men, the police! Someone had seen him enter, someone who recognized the man hunted, who summoned them. He whirled and he fled upward, softly as a fox runs, up, up until he was in the sky ballroom not yet open for the season. He forced open a door, closed it quietly after him, and he ran to the very edge of the roof, flinging himself flat in the deep shadow of a cornice. Not too soon for the lights came on in the deserted ballroom and he heard the words spoken.

"—so the service elevator's got to go on the blink when we got to finish the wiring tonight. So what do they care if we walk up. They're going to open the roof tomorrow on account of the Peace delegates——"

Withheld breath quivered from Piers. He didn't know how long he lay there while the men within hammered and thumped. After the lights were out and they went away, he lay longer. When he stood his frame ached and his head was light. Blood had caked in his hand.

He stood dark against the Broadway sky, a dwarfed figure high above the theater-bright streets. No one looked up. Not to stars, not to danger in the skies. The faces were set to the dear familiar things, the expected things. He moved unsteadily across the roof seeking a fire escape. There was none. Modern fire-stairs had eliminated their need. He had to go through the hotel again.

He shut away thinking as he entered the dark ball-room and began his long descent to escape. With his appearance he dared not take the elevator. He didn't hurry until the last flight and he turned his face from the workmen in the doorway. His arm scraped against the door as he pushed out into the street and he felt the trickle of blood again down his sleeve. He skirted through Shubert Alley, walked across to Eighth Avenue, south to 40th before doubling back to the subway entrance. In the grimy mirror of a gum vending machine, he saw himself. His mouth was swollen, discoloration marred his narrow face, his hair was torn. He smoothed the hair; there was little more he could do. His arm throbbed, blood was veining his left wrist into his palm. He held the arm close to him as he made his way to a phone booth in the underground. There could be detectives waiting for him.

He called the number Willie had given. There was no one else from whom he could seek help. He had known he wouldn't reach a cabbie at this hour of Broadway glory. Yet he had hoped. There must be a hole where he could hide until morning.

The voice at the other end of the wire said, "Well, make up your mind. You want I should tell him to call you back or don't you?"

Piers said faintly, "Where can I wait for him? How can I find him?"

"Wyncha say so before?" The voice was disgust. "If you want to see him tonight you better come up to the garage here. He'll be in sometime."

Piers repeated the address, in the West 50's, between Ninth and Tenth avenues. He climbed the stairs to the street, the 40th street exit. But his fears returned and he couldn't force himself to take the dark streets that led across to Ninth. He turned his face again to Broadway. The pain in his arm was enervating and his steps lagged into the brightness. He moved through the crowds as in a long dream. He faltered at the Astor, turning his head hungrily at the steps. Within the doorway there was the movement of beautiful women and expensive men. He was a beggar outside the gates. He could smell the luxury within, the luxury of plenty and of peace. No one knew that beauty had been slain above their heads, that peace and plenty might yet be doomed.

He walked on. Beneath the percussion of the street there crept the soft relentless sound of his pursuers.

He couldn't get away. If one step was silenced another caught up the sound. Follow, follow . . . But he wasn't to die. He was to live. To defeat ape that Man might live. He was to live to remember Morgen. *The whole fabric of the world is empty.* It must remain empty for the eternity of life. *Fate is inevitable. Ubi sunt . . . ?*

He hesitated at 49th and he leaned against the wall of the building there for a moment of strength. He dragged across the street in time to board the crosstown bus. At Ninth avenue he descended. Fear enveloped him as he stood alone there, in the desert darkness, in the silence. There were blocks he must cover to reach the garage, haunted, knowing death followed. Knowing despite the weariness that death would not reach him. He moved only because he must move; he must run from death until was accomplished what he had come to accomplish.

He kept close to the wall, feeling his way forward, not daring look back to see what might breathe against his neck. He was wet with weakness but his fear moved him, one block, another, down the endless tunnel of loneness and shadow. He watched cautiously the intersections until he saw the dark bulk of the garage half way down and across the block. He fled towards it, moving too fast now, breaking into a half run as he covered the dark street. Up three steps, and he stumbled through the open door.

A small light burned in the dingy office. There were three men there, three mongrel men. Piers tried to speak but his throat was closed.

The man with grease smudged on his stubbled chin demanded, "Whatcha want?"

Piers recognized the voice of the phone. He could speak now if hoarsely. "I want Willie."

"You the guy what called him up?"

He nodded and he put his back against the wall to steady himself. He saw a man pass the open door, disappear into the dark beyond. He began to tremble.

The smallest man with a cab-driver's cap hung over his crumpled ear rolled towards him. "Looks like you got trouble."

His speech came with difficulty. "Willie said—if trouble—come to him."

"Jeeze, he's shot!" the second cabbie said sharply.

"Nothing." He let them put him in the scarred wooden chair away from that open door. "A scratch."

The boss said, "We don't want no trouble with the cops, Mister."

"What's the matter with you, Bull?" the first cabbie demanded. "He's a friend of Willie's."

"It isn't the cops," Piers said.

"How do we know, Jack?" Bull demanded of the first cabbie in return. "We don't want no trouble."

Piers found the dirty card. "Willie gave me this."

The three examined it.

"I'm all right." As long as he was out of the dark, safe with other men. "I could use a drink. And some food. I'm hungry, that's all." Dinner seemed dreams away. He brought two tens out of his pocket. "Any place around you could get me some food and a bottle of brandy?"

Jack said, "I'll take care of it." He took the money and he went out whistling. Piers didn't know if he'd return with the police or not. If so he would have to be taken; he hadn't the strength to move.

Bull was still dubious. "You better wash your face. If the cops should be hanging around—Sammy, you show him."

Piers' head was light as he felt his way after Sammy to the miserly washroom. He splashed his face. His left arm was too stiff to move it but he washed away the blood from his hand and wrist as he could. Sammy led him back to the room. He sat down in the chair furthest from the door.

Sammy's curious eyes, Bull's suspicion watched him. He didn't care. He sat there silent until Jack returned. The little cabman was alone. He had a bucket of coffee in his hand and a sack of hamburgers. From his back pocket he took a bottle of brandy. The change clinked on the table. "There you are, Mister."

Piers opened the bottle, took a stiff slug. He passed it to the next man. He began to eat hungrily. He spoke through a mouthful, "Help yourselves. This is all I needed. I'll be all right. Willie's sure to come in?"

Bull wiped the mouth of the bottle with his forearm. "He'll be here. Maybe two o'clock—three—"

It wasn't yet one o'clock. Piers ate the second hamburger more slowly. Sanity was returning to him and courage.

Jack grinned through a bite. "How does the other guy look?"

Piers said solemnly, "I should have killed him. He tried to kill me." Death was too good for Hugo. He should suffer torment worse than death.

"What was the trouble? A woman?" The curiosity was idle.

"Yes." He cried it from the depths, "Yes. He killed her." And I killed her. She whom we loved, we have slain.

Bull's lip jutted out and he stood tall. "I told you we don't want to get mixed up in no trouble with the cops. Killing's trouble." His head jerked to the door.

Piers' fingers gripped the warped table. He spoke from his desperate need. "You can't put me out now. Willie told me to come here. He's the only one I can trust to help me. I must have help. This man is a killer."

"We don't want no Valentine massacres here." Bull's neck muscles were dark and thick. "Sorry, Mister."

Sammy squeaked as if a gun covered the room. "We'll tell Willie where to meet you. Where?"

"I have no place to go." Grayness ate into his face. "Only to death. I can't die, not yet."

Sammy's hand described what might have been a cross. Bull stood, an unyielding mass. Jack said, chewing, "Why not wait till Willie shows up?"

"You shut your face," Bull threatened. "I'm not having no cops here. Once they get on you they never get off. I know."

Piers made a last hopeless try. "Do you know who Secretary Anstruther is?"

"What's that got to do with it?"

"Do you?" he insisted.

"Who don't?" Bull said. "He's Secretary of Peace."

Piers spoke carefully, as to a child. "The man who attempted to kill me tonight, who will if he can kill me before tomorrow, is the man who murdered Secretary Anstruther."

The three faces turned to him with something like fear, fear of his madness. He met their eyes in turn hoping the truth could be seen in his through the pitiful admixture of hopelessness and fright. And then anger rose in him at their open rejection of his word. He demanded, "Do you want peace?"

"We got peace," Bull said.

"Not if Germany has her will in this Conclave. Not if the International Army is withdrawn."

"Who's that nutty?"

Piers said, "The Germans killed Secretary Anstruther." He wiped his thin hand over his forehead. "They tricked him into a plane and they shot him in the back."

There was silence. Jack rubbed his nose. "What'd they want to do that for?"

Piers saw the wink to the others, humor the madman. "Because Secretary Anstruther believed that the peace terms should be carried out as written, that Germany should remain under the protectorate for fifty years."

"And if they bump off Anstruther," Jack explained just as if he believed, "then they don't have to, is that it?"

Piers said, "That happens to be it. The man who will take the Secretary's place is friendly to Germany.

As is Lord Evanhurst, head of the English Commission."

"Where do you come in?" Bull's chin stuck out. He played the game, but grudgingly.

"I'm the man who saw the hole in Anstruther's back. I was flying after him, carrying his dispatches which he'd left behind." That was good enough. "I found him dead. The Germans know I have those papers. If they can kill me tonight, I can't present them to the Conclave tomorrow."

"There's one thing smells." Bull's mind was working. "Nobody's saying Secretary Anstruther's dead, only that there's something funny about him not turning up. If Secretary Anstruther was dead there'd be headlines all over the papers."

"There will be," Piers said. "After the Conclave. Anstruther's successor didn't want it published until after the Conclave. If it had been the delegates might not have convened. And Germany wouldn't be released from the protectorate at this time."

"Who are you, Mister?" Sammy's mouth was round and greasy.

"I'm Piers Hunt. You've never heard of me."

"I heard of you." Bull thrust forward. "You're the guy Winchell's daring to come out and talk. You heard it, Sammy, the special broadcast tonight."

Piers continued, "I've worked with Secretary Anstruther for twelve years, ever since peace was declared. In Europe and in Africa." He hesitated. "I haven't dared talk before tomorrow."

"I'm getting it," Jack nodded. "If you get bumped off you can't throw a monkey wrench tomorrow. Is that it? You're going to go to the Conclave tomorrow and tell all about Secretary Anstruther, that it?"

"That's it," Piers said. "That's why I want to live until tomorrow. To keep Germany from starting another war. If you'll only let me stay until Willie comes, he'll tell you I'm speaking true. He has seen one of the Germans who followed me."

Jack said, "Guess we'd better take in the Conclave tomorrow. Sounds like a good show."

They still didn't believe. Their interest was caught but that was all. Impassionedly he beat against their doubt. "It is important you go tomorrow. Important that you crowd the galleries with men who want peace." It didn't matter if they thought he was insane as long as they would be there. Surely they would go; they wouldn't miss finding out for themselves just how crazy this man was who declared Anstruther's death. Not these three alone, their friends and neighbors, curiosity engendered by newspaper and radio would guide them. If they would be there, even if he did die too soon, peace would have a voice. With man present, man who believed in peace, who was not afraid to demand peace, there would be peace. And he would have won no matter what happened. Watkins must be right; Man could speak.

His eyes closed. He went to sleep sitting upright there in the scarred chair, the others still asking questions. He awoke to Willie's voice. "Looks like trouble caught up. That German scrub?"

It was two-thirty in the morning. Piers said, "His boss."

Bull wasn't hostile now. Willie must have talked while Piers slept.

Willie asked, "Where you want to go, Mister?"

"I'm hiring your cab, Willie." He took out his bill-fold. "From now until tomorrow afternoon, until you deliver me at the Halls of Peace tomorrow." He counted out two hundred dollars. "Is that enough?"

Willie whistled. "You buying or renting?" He stuck the money in his pocket.

"You know it's dangerous?" Piers said.

"Where do we go?"

He said, "At eight in the morning I must be at the Thirty-third street postoffice. Until then it doesn't matter." He counted fifty dollars three times on the table. One for Bull, one for Sammy, one for Jack. Like buying votes in an election, votes for peace.

"What's that for?" Bull demanded.

"For what I've said. Fill the galleries tomorrow. Bring your friends. I want Nick Pulaski, too—he's for peace. Call him at the International Building. Tell him to bring his friends. Bring everyone who will shout for peace."

"For fifty smackers I'll fill them galleries single-handed," Sammy grinned. "How do we report to you?"

"You don't."

"Then how you know we'll be there?" Jack shook his head.

"I will know." He would know. And he'd be in the galleries with them, somehow from the galleries he too would be heard.

He turned to Willie. "I don't know where we'll hide until morning. They're on my heels now."

"We could go to my apartment," Willie said. "There's a couch where you could catch a snooze."

Bull wiped his forearm under his nose. He spoke as he folded away the fifty. "Whyncha go upstairs and lie down in my room till morning? If you go home, Willie, you'll never make it back in time. Not the way you sleep. I'll wake you when I go off duty at seven."

"What you say, Mister?" Willie pursed his mouth.

Piers said, "I'd be grateful." Grateful for any place to lay his head, for a little rest, for not having to step out into the terrors of the night again.

"It ain't fancy," Bull apologized. "Not very clean. I'm not much hand at housekeeping."

"It is safe?" Piers hesitated.

"Nobody can get up there without getting by me." There were knots in his powerful arms. He led the way up the iron staircase into the loft of parked cars. The sleeping room was half as big as the office. Bull said, "You can lie on the cot. Willie, you fix up the chairs for yourself."

The window was small, looking down to an alley. No one could climb the blank wall. Someone was shadowed in the alley waiting. Piers drew back. He moved to the cot and he sat down.

Bull said, "You'll be safe. I'll wake you at seven."

"Thanks more than I can say."

Bull went out. Piers said, "Push your chair against the door, Willie."

"Scared?"

He nodded. He winced as he lay down.

"You ought to have a doctor look at that arm. Don't pay to let them go. Infection's bad. My brother-in-law—"

"Tomorrow." He closed his eyes. No one could get by Bull. No one could get by Willie in the chair. No one could climb through the little window. But his dreams were troubled and he walked on the top of the waters of sleep.

4.

He heard the knocking while Willie snored on. He jerked up. "Who is it?"

"Seven o'clock. You guys in there, it's seven o'clock."

Piers said, "We're up." He said, "Come on, Willie. We have to move on now." His clothes looked as if they'd been slept in; every bone, not only the wounded one, ached.

Willie yawned. "Jeeze," he said. "I forgot to call the wife." He opened the door to Bull. "I forgot to call Mame. She'll be maddern a wet hen."

"Two hundred smackers'll get her over the mad fast." Bull led them down the stairs to the washroom.

Piers rubbed the stubble on his chin, met his tired eyes in the scrap of mirror. He must find some place today to bathe and shave, to have his clothes pressed. He wondered wearily what tale Hugo had told, if now he himself was wanted for murder other than presumptive. It didn't matter. If he won peace, his truth would be good. If he lost it, nothing mattered.

He combed back his hair, straightened his tie. "If you know a quick place and a safe one, we'll have coffee before we go downtown."

Bull cleared his throat gruffly. "You guys don't need some help, do you?"

"Thanks again." Piers took his hand. "We'll get along." He wouldn't involve anyone else in what might be violence. Willie at the wheel of the cab should be out of the line of danger. "Just be sure not to miss the Conclave today."

"I wouldn't miss it." It was a threat.

The cab was inside the storage garage. Piers got in the back seat; it would be safer for the driver in case—

"We going to be followed today?" Willie turned on the ignition.

"I hope not." He mustn't be followed this morning.

"Hold on to your hat then."

The cab shot out of the garage. Piers slumped in the seat holding the strap clenched to his right hand. He didn't know the neighborhood where they stopped for coffee. He only knew the taste was good. They started off again, carving a curling path through the city. Seventh Avenue was quiet on this early morning, this Sunday spring morning. Piers asked as they neared the Pennsylvania station, "Anyone following?"

"Not as I can see." Willie wasn't so certain now. "You got me so jittery I thought I seen a cab after we left the Coffee Cup. That's why I cut over to the river."

"I want to pick up my mail." Piers spoke hushedly as if here in the rolling cab someone might overhear.

"It's Sunday."

"I have a box." His heart had begun to thud. This was the moment, the act that must be kept inviolate. From the rear window he could see no approaching car. He said, "You stay in the cab. Keep the engine running."

"If that fat Heinie turns up?"

He hesitated too long. He couldn't say, Call the police; he would be no better off in the hands of the law than in the hands of Germany. Not with Gordon directing the law. Perhaps the way to the end would be less cruel but the end of both was defeat, ultimate destruction. He ordered, "If there's trouble, run for it."

"What you think I am—a yellow-belly?"

"Run for it," Piers' voice rang. "And go to the Conclave. Demand peace. Make them give you peace."

He slipped from the cab door and vanished into the postoffice. He moved quickly, selecting the key from its safe hiding place among the many on his key ring, opening the box, taking out the two harmless-looking envelopes. He could hear men walking on the pavement outside, not many, casual steps. He thrust the envelopes into his inner pocket, took a breath before he stepped out to the pavement again and started to the cab.

There was no sound of a shot. The bullet stopped him. Anger rushed into him. His meeting in Samarra might have waited a few more hours. To be this close to achievement. His eyes seared. He heard Willie's

shout as he tried to force himself forward to the cab.
Willie wasn't at the wheel. Willie was running across
the street, shouting. There were many voices shouting
and he was falling, falling from a great height into
an abyss.

He heard the soft speech. "It's my boss, Mister.
He's been sick. I got the car right over there."

He opened his eyes. Sight was blurred but not beyond recognition of the dark face bending over him.
He tried to cry out but no sound would come. The
silken voice spoke on while the words faded out. The
voice was the voice of David. The irony of it smote
him. Now he would be taken to Fabian.

VIII

He wasn't dead. In death he wouldn't be lying in a clean bed; he wouldn't be fired by pain; he wouldn't see the inscrutable face of David watching from the chair.

Piers said, "Well, you've won." His voice sounded far away.

The face awoke. "You are conscious. That is good. Don't try to rise. You have lost much blood from the two wounds. The second shot was near the lung. But if you are careful—"

Piers didn't try to move. The effort of speech was trial enough. "You have the papers?"

"Yes. The photostatic copies of Secretary Anstruther's. The letters of Hugo von Eynar."

He said bitterly, "You didn't give up, did you? You kept following, following, all those days and nights."

"I knew you must retrieve the papers before the Conclave opened. You sent them to yourself, to a post box?"

"You know I did."

"Wise. You didn't go near the box until it was essential."

Piers remembered suddenly and he started to rise up. Pain wrenched him and he again lay quiet. "What is today?"

"Sunday. The same Sunday. It is noon."

Noon to sundown. And he a prisoner. He asked, "Will you let me see Fabian now?"

The man answered simply, "I am Fabian."

Piers turned his head on the pillow.

"I am David and I am Fabian. Fabian is the man of state. My people need me among them, one of them, and I am also David."

"But Fabian—Fabian is big, a giant of a man. I've seen him in Conclave. You are smaller, older—"

The man smiled. "You know theater, Piers Hunt. A robe—a headdress—the illusion of grandeur. I have always been grateful to Lord Evanhurst for his design for the robe of the Peace Commissioners."

Piers closed his eyes. "I wanted to talk with you. As a friend. In peace. You came with a gun. Today you used the gun. Why?"

Fabian was unsmiling. "I did not shoot you. It was the German."

"You didn't shoot?"

Fabian said with righteous anger, "I am a man of peace. True, I carried a gun the night I came to you. Because I believed you had killed my friend. My people found him there in the unmarked grave. I took him to a better place, he and the unknown, that no one would know his defeat and shame. I knew you had followed his plane. I believed you were working with the Germans. I could not afford to die. My people cannot go forward as yet without me. With An-

233

struther gone I must help maintain peace. I have learned since you did not kill him."

"I didn't kill him," Piers said. "But I did send him to his death."

"You cannot blame yourself."

"I let him go on the summons of that telegram—a telegram I distrusted. I should have made inquiries before I let him go."

"Could you stop him? He knew I would not call on him but in need. They who sent the telegram knew that."

"After he flew out I saw the Arab with Anstruther's case. I took it. I thought he'd stolen it. I should have known then he wasn't a sneak thief."

A sneak thief would have dropped it and fled. He wouldn't have fought to hold onto it, looking wildly for help which did not dare materialize.

"I took off in a borrowed monoplane at once. To follow. I knew the Secretary would need the African reports I had gathered for him. My plane was faster than the one he'd taken. I could overtake him when his stopped to refuel."

He had overtaken it before then, grounded in the desert. And Anstruther dead, laid on the sand. The grave had already been dug.

"I don't think he knew. The shot was in the back. They must have rigged up the gun to fire at a particular moment. The pilot wouldn't have had time to dig the grave. The body was still warm. He'd taken the Secretary's watch and ring."

To carry back to Schern, the pelt, to prove that the

Secretary was dead. With his bare hands, Piers killed the German, Gundar Abersohn. He had dug the second grave, fired the plane with the substitute case inside. He had stood there and watched the memorial pyre burn for a man of peace destroyed by violence.

He had waited until there were only black shards to show where a plane had lighted. It wasn't until later in the night, alone in his despair, knowing that peace on earth had again been banished, that he realized he alone knew Anstruther was dead. No one could know that until he told.

"I alone held the secret," he said to Fabian. "The Germans planned his death but until Abersohn reported to them that the deed was accomplished, they couldn't know. And Abersohn could never tell. It was then I photographed Anstruther's papers. The Germans would be looking for a bulky package, not a small envelope. I destroyed the originals. I destroyed the briefcase. I sent the envelope to George Thompson, general delivery, New York. I flew to Berne, made arrangements for my work to be taken over. When I reached New York I rented the box under the Thompson name, sent instructions to forward my mail from general delivery to the number. Later I sent the von Eynar papers to the same box. I didn't know I was to be followed, but if I were, the hiding place of the papers would not be given away. I didn't once go to it."

"You were followed but no one, not even I, knew soon enough that you were in New York. It was not known until Gordon learned through Berne."

"But today—no one could have followed today."

"From the garage? I did. I waited all night. And I knew where you must go."

He didn't understand. "How could you know?"

"Your papers must have been in a lock box. The banks are not open on Sunday. It must be a postoffice. There were only two to watch. I had a man at the Lexington Avenue one but I myself chanced the Pennsylvania. It is the main one and it was the more convenient for you."

And the Germans did the same; or they knew with their precise research methods. Knowing, they couldn't take the material; they had to wait for him; the mails were safe. They had waited. He asked, "Who fired the shot?"

"The fat one. The one you knocked down last night. His orders today must have been to kill; he didn't attempt to take the papers. You are fortunate that he was across the street, a bit too far for perfect marksmanship."

Yes, to kill. Because Morgen was dead. Because there was no longer time for treaties. Piers must be dead before the conference began.

"Your cabman caught him, held him for the police."

He remembered. "How did you get me away from the police?"

"Before they came I took you away. I told the onlookers I was your serving-man. They did not know you were wounded. I made them believe that it was a fight between the cabbie and the gunman. That you were an innocent bystander."

236

His bloody room at the Astor. He didn't know how to say it. "Am I wanted—have you seen the papers—is there a murder charge—"

"It is being silenced until after the Conclave closes. I have no doubt you will be arrested for the murder of Secretary Anstruther when you are found."

Morgen's death was yet unknown. Silenced by Hugo for his own purposes. "The Conclave." Again he tried to lift up. "I must be there."

"Lie quietly if you please. You are not out of danger."

"That doesn't matter. I must be there. Don't you understand? The overture to war will be played to-day."

"I understand." His voice was deep as the sound of a gong and as sad. "All are against us. The east in courtesy will not rule contrary to the will of the west. They do not see. I have pleaded with them. I have told them: It is my land that first will be stricken. The black man will again be put on all fours. They promise they will come to my assistance if we are attacked. That will mean global war anew."

The war of extermination. The end of the world.

"They will not counter the will of Secretary Anstruther. What is decided by America will be their decision."

And they will believe that Gordon speaks with the voice of Anstruther. That had been arranged.

"I have even gone to Lord Evanhurst. He scoffs at the idea of attack. He too promises help in case. Even if the promise is kept, it means war."

"Yes. And Gordon?"

Fabian said, "I did not go to Gordon."

"He could not help you." Piers understood. Gordon believed the unholy German three too well.

Fabian was speaking. "I could not beg from the murderer of my friend."

Piers looked into his eyes. "Gordon?"

"Only three men knew that the Secretary would come to you in North Africa. You who sent for him, himself, and his home secretary, Gordon."

"Gordon could have given the information away." The secret information.

"It was Gordon who ordered the telegram sent to Anstruther; it was Gordon who paid for the plane, who hired the German from a list supplied by Schern."

He tried to understand. Not the German hands guiding Gordon; Gordon behind the Germans. And yet behind Gordon the Germans again. Without their wish, he could not have been motivated. It was as a curve in time; all were together. He cried from the depths, "Why?"

"Ambition is a greedy god."

"But why didn't you tell me this—that night you came to my room?"

"I did not know. Only after you told me of the telegram did I send my men to seek the truth. By the time they discovered these things, it was too late. It was a matter of too little time. Your President had already named Gordon to succeed the Secretary."

"And you did nothing," Piers accused.

Fabian said, "What chance had I? Fabian of Equatorial Africa, suspect and accused of border troubles, to discredit the President of the United States of America? I have lived a long time, Piers Hunt, long enough to know that the will and the wish are not enough, behind them must be the power."

"You are afraid." Piers spoke from despair. "You as all the others are afraid to speak. Maybe you have lived too long under the apes. You have lost faith in man." He cried out, "Maybe I haven't lived long enough to be afraid—or maybe my little span has been so long that I have gone beyond caring for fear. I only know that I'm not afraid to speak for peace, to fight for peace. Too late? It can't be too late."

It hurt to breathe.

"You ask what I can do? I'll tell you. I am going before the Conclave today. Don't shake your head. Call in your doctors. They can give me something to put me on my feet long enough for that."

"I didn't shake my head for that, Piers Hunt. I've seen wounded men accomplish the superhuman before. I was a doctor in the Last War. I shook my head because there will be hundreds of police detectives and government officers waiting for you. They will expect you to try to attend the conference. You will be arrested before you can enter the hall."

Piers twisted a smile. "That's your part, Fabian. You will get me into the hall. You know the theater? The ceremonial robes—the headdress. My face won't be seen. No one will look for my face there."

Light lifted Fabian's eyes, the light of hope.

"Once inside I will go to the galleries, among the men. The men who aren't afraid, who will fight with me for peace."

Fabian said, "No. There can be a better way. The robes, the headdress, yes. But I am to speak this afternoon. It is the sop to Cerberus, flung by Lord Evanhurst. I speak in memory of my absent friend, Secretary Anstruther. I will offer in my stead a man of my peace commission. I will give you to them. They will not dare demean the dignity of the Conclave by moving against you while you are speaking. They will not dare insult me by moving against my man. The law will wait. You will speak what you wish to say, without fear."

It wasn't words; now he wasn't afraid. It was for this he had endured, to speak with the voice of Anstruther. Fabian said with sadness, "I do not know how much a heart can endure. I do not answer for your tomorrow."

"I am not going to die." No fear, no trepidation. "If I should, it wouldn't matter. Peace alone matters now." Not man, nor woman; not life, nor death.

Fabian handed him a glass. "Drink this and rest. I will come for you in time."

Piers gulped the draught.

Fabian went to the door. "I have been afraid," he said. "My faith was small. I thought that Anstruther's death meant the torch had been extinguished. I did not know a hand would grasp it as it fell."

2.

The International Halls of Peace rose tall and white on the Palisades. As the great windows flamed with the setting sun, the delegates gathered in the circular chamber. They could never come together here without remembering Anstruther. The poet in him had planned the majesty of the gathering, the hour of sunset; the blue flag of peace, marked with the white winged dove, the sturdy olive tree, blowing triumphantly. The room was filled with sound and majesty. The blue robes of America, the royal purple of Britain, the red of Russia, the gold of China, all the spectrum represented in all the nations of the world. The great four were in their predominant places. Gordon, handsome in his dress despite the tension lines about his mouth. The Germans had entered. Brecklein's face was heavy, Schern's head darted like an adder. Hugo's bruises were cosmetized but no one had painted a smile on his face.

Piers had passed unnoticed into the hall at Fabian's side. The scarlet robe he wore, the envoy's hood, made his face of no importance as he had planned. His tan was deeper color than some of Fabian's other men.

The open galleries were massed with the faces of men. Without the grounds were massed with those for whom there was no room within, waiting to hear without seeing, waiting to know the fate of the world, of peace. There was no fright on their faces; there was curiosity and beneath it decision. Piers turned his eyes upward seeking faces with names, Willie, Bull, Jack, Sammy, Nick Pulaski, even Cassidy. They were there. They must be there. Tonight peace would be on earth.

He had no weakness at the moment. When there

was no consciousness of body there could be no pain. The fire of strength that inflamed him overcame all else. He waited tensed and sure, as sure as Gordon had been a few sundowns ago.

The bells of the Conclave rang out. The invocation was spoken, the words echoed in the hall, "Peace be with thee, And with thy spirit."

Lord Evanhurst stood awaiting silence. Thin and old, yes, but empurpled, his delicate face showing no trace of the clever brain behind it. His dignity carried to the furthest corner of the hall. "It is with the greatest regret that I bring you word that our Secretary will not be able to attend the present conclave." He waited but the reaction was minute. The press didn't stir; the story was in type, awaiting only deadline release. Only to the least important nations could this be information, and even they must have been fed by the grapevine. "The President of the United States has named the first secretary to Secretary Anstruther, De Witt Gordon, to act in his place. Secretary Gordon will assume the chair."

Gordon came forward. The applause was not of their knowledge of him, it was for his stature. He spoke. Words, brave words, stirring words, no apologies, no hint of the anxieties wracking him. Time enough for that tomorrow when the business was begun. Nothing must mar today, not even the knowledge that Piers Hunt was in freedom.

He finished speaking in tumult and shouting. The relief on his face was pitiful. He had been accepted. He raised his arms. "At the suggestion of the dean of our members, Lord Evanhurst, I have asked a man whom Secretary Anstruther calls friend to speak to you of our beloved and absent leader. Secretary Fabian of Equatorial Africa."

The delegations were without interest. Another speech. The opening of the Conclave, pretty speeches, pageantry, no more. Nothing of import at the ceremonial overture. But the galleries were agape. They had come for the show; they would suck this orange to the fullest. They knew what the delegations had forgotten. Every moment for peace could be important.

The emphasis of eyes shifted from the stalls of the mighty to the faraway position of the new African nation. Fabian rose, majestic, commanding. Even the delegates were forced into attention as he stood there waiting for the murmur of applause to subside. Mouths bent to ears, the rustle of sound. This is Fabian, the mystic, the guarded, the enigmatic.

Fabian lifted his hands. "Peace be among us." It was a prayer, not a catch phrase of the Conclave, a prayer more powerful than the perfunctory obsequy which had opened the meeting. It was torn from the black man's hope. He waited until its overtones faded into the high dome.

"I have been asked to speak to you of Secretary Anstruther, our Secretary, my beloved friend. I cannot speak to you of my friend. When the heart is heavy with grief the mouth is filled only with silence."

There was the first faint wind of doubt blown across the heads of the mighty. Gordon's hand lifted and fell, but Evanhurst did not move. Only his lips were finer drawn than before. Among the Germans there was the shifting of eyes. The hall was silent as Fabian's voice softened.

"I can speak of our Secretary but there is no reason for me to speak of him. You knew him. You knew he was a gentle man, a good man, a just man." The clangor of iron rang in his words. "Secretary Anstruther is dead."

There was no sound from the delegates in their marble stalls. The first rumble of distant thunder came from the galleries alone. The guilty ones dared not stir.

"Because he was just, his death demands that justice be fulfilled. Because he was just, his assassins must be brought before justice. Secretary Anstruther was murdered."

The thunder grew. The Germans looked for escape but there was no escape here. Man was watching from above, man waited without. Gordon's eyes were holes in the clay of his face. On Evanhurst's mouth there moved a smile but his thin fingers were wound tight about the arms of his chair.

"I cannot tell you how he was murdered. I do not know. I found his body with the one who was the instrument of death. I carried both to the Lake of the Crocodiles that the killer might be destroyed even unto his ash, that my friend might rest where his goodness is enshrined, where his peace will be preserved."

They were losing fear, the guilty ones. Brecklein's fingertips came together. Sly hope crept over them. Hugo put up his eyeglass.

"My friend is gone. And when I knew that he was gone, I was afraid. I knew he was not killed because he was gentle, although his gentleness betrayed him to his enemies. He was not killed because he was good, although his goodness was a threat to them. He was not killed because he was just, for being a just man he was not quick to accuse. He was killed because he was a man of peace. And I was afraid. I thought with him peace too had died, as his assassins meant peace should die. In my fear I believed these things. Until today.

"Today a man proved to me that I was wrong. Peace is not dead because peace must not die. This man can speak not of Secretary Anstruther but for him. Better than I he can speak to you for my friend. Because he was the better friend. Because he believed when I knew only doubt and fear."

His hand gestured Piers to his feet. "I give you Piers Hunt."

Piers spoke while the moment held. His voice throbbed into the hall. "I speak for Secretary Anstruther."

He didn't wait for them to gather their forces to strike him down, for despite Fabian's belief to the contrary, they would strike even here in the sanctum of peace if given opportunity.

"Secretary Anstruther labored for peace. Secretary Anstruther believed in peace. Secretary Anstruther wanted only peace. Because he was a man of peace, he is dead."

He didn't know how much he dared say. He didn't know how much truth he dared put into the massive hands that knotted above. Truth was the powerful weapon. Throughout the history of the world it had been withheld from man as too dangerous for his manipulations. Piers would not fear man, he could not. Man alone could save the world. The truth must not be confined to the chosen; it must be given all. He must speak now or Anstruther and that for which he stood went down into darkness forever.

He knew and man must know. They must look back and see one man alone in the jungle of the past daring to aspire to the dignity of man, neither to ape the apes nor to be satisfied with the brutish natural state of man. How many men must have been done away with both by the apes and his fellow brutes before the achievement? But the achievement came to be. The apes still swung by their tails but tails were no longer the shape of nobility. The luxurious ape, the aristo-cratic ape, the darling ape, the delicate ape was legend and dust. One man aspiring raised all men above the apes.

Man must be made to remember what aspiring man forgot when the achievement was forgotten as an achievement, when it was granted; remember that the brutish spirit remained dormant in too many of his brothers. They no longer clubbed their thrust-jawed, jut-browed way through the jungle. They had taken on the outward accouterments of dignified man but within the brute instinct roiled. Man must remember anew what man dignified as man forgot, that there would always be those others who could not forget the graces and luxuries of the delicate ape, who would, after having forgotten the pattern, ape the ape. It was the brutes who waged the wars; it was the apes who instigated them, swinging from their safe high-leaved trees.

As these atavists could not be bred out of the race, neither could men of aspiration, men who watched neither the earth nor the trees, whose eyes lifted to the stars and beyond.

Thus he spoke and there was silence while he thus spoke. His words went on out of his hard anger and determination. He saw the rage and frustration beginning to cover the faces of the Germans, the fearful defeat on Gordon's shoulders, the ironic acceptance of reversal in Lord Evanhurst's smile.

And his anger grew and he spewed out the entire truth. "I accuse the guilty ones and I say to you in Fabian's hands is the proof of their guilt. There is proof in a telegram which forged the name of Fabian. There is proof in a man hired to pilot a death plane. There is proof in the murdered body of Anstruther— a bullet hole in his back. They will say they did not kill. That is true. Their hands are not soiled with blood. Their hands only forged the tool that would slay."

His voice rang harshly, "I accuse them by nation— Germany. I accuse them by name—Brecklein, Schern, von Eynar."

The three did not believe this. Their heads jerked and they started to rise. They shrank again in their chairs as he cried out, "Stand! Stand and deny!— what you cannot deny."

247

His voice quieted to scorn. "And I accuse the Judas who sold his friend not for thirty pieces of silver but for the robe he wears—De Witt Gordon."

The fear and shame on Gordon's face was terrible to see. Piers turned his eyes away from it. "I accuse all those who have threatened peace by dealing with these men."

The anger was gone. "Secretary Anstruther died for peace. Because he had decreed that no nation and no individual within any nation should threaten peace."

Behind Evanhurst he saw Watkins' strong shoulders, shoulders waiting for burden, willing to accept it. He saw Mancianargo, and the way his whipped eyes lighted in hope as the interpreter whispered to the Italian peasant. He saw incredulous tears on the cheeks of the French Dessaye. He saw faith replacing fear under the flag of Czecho-Slovakia, of Poland, of Finland, of Greece, of all nations who had suffered and died and risen again from hell.

"Secretary Anstruther was murdered by men and nations who despise the equality of peace. I give you that proof now, not to the few in secret session, but now to all men of peace. You shall decide the rewards of the guilty."

There was no doubt where Asia would take stand. Justice stood awful on the brows of her nations. As Fabian went, now would go the conference.

"Anstruther is dead but his words are not dead." He held the sheaf of papers high in his hand for all to look upon. If he was shot down now, the papers were safe. "I bring you his last work, the words he entrusted to me."

They were open accusation. They were Piers' findings of the border incidents, and they were the simple familiar tale of treachery against a man who was a man of peace, who could not be swerved from right and decency and the good. He would not hurry these words, each syllable must be heard by all present. He was weakening now, the drugs with which Fabian had bolstered him were wearing thin and pain had reawakened, spearing him. He didn't falter. The men without power, the men with voice and will alone, the Nicks and Willies and Bulls, must hear; there must be no chance for the schemers to scheme again, to threaten, to harry and bribe, to offer counter-proposal. He read until the last paper alone was in his hand, and he leaned against the podium.

"This was written in the plane, the plane piloted by that German officer, purchased by that American friend, the plane in which he was given death, a shot in the back. I read you the last words of Anstruther."

He read:

"Without peace, our world ends. There can be no peace unless we are strong enough, courageous enough, to deny our weakness. It would be weakness for us to turn back from what we know is right."

No one could doubt that these were the words of Anstruther. No one among the nations but had heard him so speak. No one would ever know that Piers Hunt had on that despairing night, on his return from the desert, forged this last paper.

He read the final line: "Germany must continue to be protected in accordance with our agreed plan for peace."

He clenched the podium. His eyes lifted to the faces of the men, his voice cried, "Anstruther died for peace. Do you want peace?"

He waited, heard the first whisper, the echo, "Peace."

He cried again, louder now, "Do you want peace?"

The echo repeated more strongly, "Peace. Peace."

His sight was blurring but his fingers dug into the stand and he remained upright. "Do you want Peace? *Do you want Peace?*"

He heard the swelling from above, from below, from without, "Peace . . . Peace . . . Peace . . ."

Fabian's hand caught his arm, supported him. He saw from far away Evanhurst and Gordon opening empty mouths, their words silent under the chant for peace. He saw the graven images of Germany. He alone heard the mocking voice of dissent, "Melodrama, Piers?" He alone answered, "Any weapon for peace, Morgen. Even death."

The Conclave would dare not turn against the cry of man, rising to frenzy now, to grandeur. This time he had won. But he knew the fight must be fought over and again, each year, each day, each minute. The beast would snarl anew, the delicate ape would scheme. Man must fight on until peace was as fixed on the earth as the stars were fixed in the cosmos.

The room was fading but the magnificat of the chant swelled to a roar, "Peace . . ." He saw Fabian's face, strong, smiling. As Piers crumpled, he smiled too.

THE END

>>> If you've enjoyed this book and would like to discover more great vintage crime and thriller titles, as well as the most exciting crime and thriller authors writing today, visit: >>>

The Murder Room
Where Criminal Minds Meet

themurderroom.com

www.ingramcontent.com/pod-product-compliance
Ingram Content Group UK Ltd.
Pitfield, Milton Keynes, MK11 3LW, UK
UKHW022317280225
455674UK00004B/346

9 781471 917332